THE ARCHITECTURE OF FEAR

Sandro William Junqueira

THE ARCHITECTURE OF FEAR

Translated from the Portuguese by
Ángel Gurría-Quintana

First published in Portugal as *Um Piano Para Cavalos Altos* in 2012 by Editorial Caminho

First published in the English language in 2025 by
Mountain Leopard Press
An imprint of Headline Publishing Group Limited

1

Cataloguing in Publication Data is available from the British Library

ISBN (HB) 978 1 9144 9597 7

Typeset in 12/15.5pt Sabon LT Std by Jouve (UK), Milton Keynes

Printed and bound in Great Britain by Clays Ltd, Elcograf S.p.A.

HEADLINE PUBLISHING GROUP LIMITED
An Hachette UK Company
Carmelite House
50 Victoria Embankment
London EC4Y 0DZ

The authorised representative in the EEA is Hachette Ireland, 8 Castlecourt Centre,
Dublin 15, D15 XTP3, Ireland (email: info@hbgi.ie)

www.headline.co.uk
www.hachette.co.uk

For Catarina, for Guilherme
For the fish in the tank

When a person is born, he can embark on only one
*   of three roads of life:*
if you go right, the wolves will eat you;
if you go left, you'll eat the wolves;
if you go straight, you'll eat yourself.

Anton Chekhov
Platonov

Contents

WINTER SONATA

The soothsaying leg (I)

At the edge of the Forest, the soldiers tug at the reins. The three horses are forced to stop. They bury their hoofs in the mute snow. They neigh. The soldiers glance at one another. One of them spits.

The soldier who spat looks ahead with determination and does not hesitate even though his right leg is aching. His right leg always aches whenever he approaches something too large to be seen by eyes alone. He calls it the *soothsaying leg.*

Life had taught this soldier enough to put his trust in a lame leg, and not harbour any illusions in his heart.

He clears his throat, cups his hands around his mouth and shouts towards the Forest. The other two soldiers add their dissonant voices to the shout. The shout has a name: despair. It leaves their hoarse throats, repeatedly. It echoes beyond the branches. The Forest does not reply. Not even the owls.

There is a roughness in the air. The cold hurts. It slaps with an open hand. The three horses are on edge. Breath streams out of their enlarged nostrils, rises. Their bulging eyes cannot stay still.

What now? asks one of the soldiers.

I'm not going in there, another says.

We can't disobey orders. He'll show up, replies the third, the soldier with the determined gaze, the one with the *soothsaying leg.* After a pause, he sniffs the air and continues.

Nothing to worry about. We've got our guns.

Bullets tickle the *Devil*.

What *Devil*? Don't be stupid. It's just the Forest. Just trees growing very closely together.

It's *His* territory.

I told you: we need to find him. If not, there'll be hell to pay.

One of the soldiers shakes his head.

The Messenger was going around town saying that the wolves . . .

The Messenger is crazy. He'll be locked up, the Lame Soldier says, trying to bring the conversation to a close.

He spits again.

Although he has few certainties about the matter, only suspicions, he speaks with great conviction. Four silver bars glisten on his shoulders: hierarchical power.

The Lame Soldier tugs at the reins. He digs his officer's spurs into his horse's ribs. The others do the same and follow him, concerned.

The crow cawed twice

Light from the torches sways in the soldiers' hands as they search for a trail of footprints. The horses move forward, slowly, zig-zagging to avoid obstacles. The soldiers can see only night between the branches, how everything is empty.

In the summer it was easy to tell the firs, the beeches, the birches, the pines. But now, in deepest winter: only a labyrinth of blackened tree trunks connecting the snow to the grey clouds.

The crow cawed as it saw them approach the clearing. It flew off the ground. It beat its wings towards the roof of the abandoned cottage. In its hard beak it carried a piece of flesh. It landed on the roof next to the sealed-off chimney. It remained there, observing the men.

The three soldiers dismounted close to the red snow. As the clouds cleared, the moon shone through and lit up the clearing. The Lame Soldier walked with pain biting his leg like a dog. Heavy step, light step. He pointed his torch. He walked around the corpse but could not smell death. The cold had crystallised the offensive stench. The other two soldiers, numbed, a few metres behind, did not let go of the reins: their excuse was having to look after the horses.

Once again, his right leg was not wrong. There it was: *the big thing.* The lost soldier, torn to strips. He was missing his hands, his nose, his ears, his eyes, part of a leg and a foot. Eviscerated, his abdomen an empty cavity. He was recognisable only by the shreds of his uniform and the metal star, the symbol of Government, hard and impossible to digest and therefore spared the jaws of violence.

There was no more body to speak of, no wholeness.

A cruel wind howls from the northern-facing mountains. It sounds like a violin being tuned. It blows through the rows of tree trunks, the stiff pine needles and all that cold.

Despite the horror of the situation, the Lame Soldier noted how beautiful the reddened snow looked. Blood looks good against the white, he thought.

Finally, and after the crow had cawed once again, he turned towards the reluctant soldiers. He shouted:

It's him. We found him.

Spine-tingling news

It did not take long for the wind of news to spread across the City.

From mouth to ear, from ear to mouth, people excitedly shared different versions of events, as always happens with hearsay and tittle-tattle. Each person added some personal seasoning to the story.

There was talk of nothing else. Everyone nodded and shook their heads. They sighed. They proclaimed. Mouths brimming with tales:

The wolves killed a soldier in the Forest!

A holocaust!

That wasn't the work of wolves, it was the work of the *Devil*!

The Messenger saw it in a dream and warned us, and now it's happened!

They bit off his feet, hands and eyes!

A bear woke up from its winter sleep, that's what really happened!

For people in the City, the excitement about the tragedy was understandable. It had been some ten years since anyone talked about things happening in the Forest. Other than in the summer, when people might comment on the arrival of insects and berries, or the wildfires, when from a distance they spied the ugly columns of smoke, the dark smell. Despite the fear caused by the spine-tingling news, in some hearts there was a new splinter of happiness, enthusiasm. The unexpected event offered a glimpse onto a new landscape. A door opening onto a new darkness.

When the Bald Minister gets angry and takes measures

The Government, always cautious, had this time been unable to keep the story under wraps and deny the threat. A young soldier had, indeed, been the victim of an unusual attack deep in the Forest. And the strangeness of the death rattled the top brass, unwilling to admit the weakness of the armed forces when they ventured far beyond the Wall and into nature.

In the Government Tower, upon hearing the news, the Bald Minister banged his fist on the table. He roared at his advisors:

Unacceptable. Soldiers can and must die, but in combat; fighting for their flag; against an armed enemy. Not killed by the teeth of beasts, of uncivilised things. To bleed without fighting is for cowards.

After his outburst, the Bald Minister made a quick decision:

We'll send another armed regiment into the Forest with this mission: to kill everything they find that they cannot tame. I want blood and pelts to cover every District in the City. So that people stop imagining things and spreading tales.

Seventeen days later, the regiment returned, exhausted, saddlebags empty of rations and hands trembling. The men's hands trembled because they were cold, but also because they were afraid. Despite their different natures, both cold and fear make hands tremble.

The column of soldiers crossed one of the Wall's metal gates, and on the horses' flanks there were no pelts dripping in blood. This hunting expedition, like others before it, had resulted in a big nothing. Nature knows when to be still. And when to hide its teeth.

It was not the first time that a regiment returning from the Forest crossed the Wall with empty and trembling hands. Faced with a new failure, the Bald Minister, trying to calm the people's restless hearts and wagging tongues, had no choice but to order the arrest of a worker from the Factory's north wing. The Bald Minister conceived the idea and shared it with his advisors:

If we can't kill the howling wolves, we can at least silence the bleating lamb.

This lamb that bleated and unsettled the rest of the flock was, the Bald Minister said, an unusual man in whom many people recognised mystic or prophetic powers. And those powers were giving him an inconvenient prominence. He made the authorities nervous. That worker had the gift of dreaming things that had not yet happened but would in all certainty happen. He dreamed about things and events that, later, happened with irritating inevitability.

He carried within him the fearsome mystery of knowing.

He was the man that everyone called the Messenger.

Holocaust at the altar (I):
The spat-upon pray

They gathered in the basement of one of the Brown Zone's estates. Men, women. Those that destiny had mercilessly spat on. The *spat-upon* were there to listen.

Rows of candlesticks with lit candles lined the path to the pulpit. At the back, burlap sacks filled with barley and wheat made the basement look like a bunker and smell like a granary.

The weak candlelight played hide-and-seek. Trembling shadows on dirty walls. On the expectant faces in profile. Shadows went and came.

Men, women, mouths puckered, eyes fixed on their shoes, nostrils contracting as they breathed in. As if breathing were an unseemly act. Sat on old fruit boxes, they mumbled through the litany: a current of quick words pressed against their teeth and washed by their tongues.

At the far end of the basement, on the stage, the Messenger conducted the prayer from behind a pulpit made of crates. Stiff, chin jutting, arms open: a ventriloquist's dummy. He rejoiced in the collective ecstasy. The euphoric prayer licked the *spat-upon* like a greedy dog.

The Messenger shouted out the final word, which was echoed by the congregation.

Repeated by many mouths, the breath of that final word

blew out the candles' restless flames. The Messenger opened his eyes. He unlocked hands and turned to the crowd. A murmur swept through the congregation. Shadows grew. A brouhaha of astonishment. And then: silence and darkness. The audience understood something miraculous was happening: *He* was there. Among the men, and the women.

They lowered their eyes as a sign of devotion. They felt closer to him without the distraction of sight. The Messenger's pupils dilated in the dark, like cats' pupils when they hunt at night. He joined his hands over his breastbone, entwined his fingers, swallowed, and then started.

The buttery voice, speaking in old words, lofty; he moved around the basement like an experienced dancer.

From that moment the Messenger's voice became a light in the dark.

A moon full of words.

Holocaust at the altar (II): When I said turn left, they turned right

The Messenger said:

Brothers and Sisters. May *He* bless your light and wash away the fear that has grown in your hearts. *He* is the witness and is among us. *He* knows, and *He* is among us. Tonight, *He* will speak to you. It's what *He* wants. Last night, *He* appeared in my dreams in the shape of an angel. *He* spoke through the angel. In the dream, *He* spoke words without having spoken the words. Words are wasted in the mouths of men, *He* said. And in the dream, *He* spoke of what has not yet happened but will happen for certain. Let me tell you what *He* said:

Soon the trees will spill blood onto the snow.
    The spilt blood will have a pleasant odour.
    The wolves will sniff the scent in the distance.
    The blood-stained snow will announce that the time of the holocaust has arrived.
    He also said:
    The wolves will come, and they will know the wicked, and they will drink the blood of the wicked.
    And *He* repeated:
    The wolves will come, and they will know the wicked, and they will drink the blood of the wicked.
    And *He* continued:

Fear not the beasts with sharpened teeth and jaws dripping with pestilent slobber.

Fear not those that feed on hot flesh because their blood commands them to.

Wolves are not the real wolves.

The real wolves are those surrounding you in the guise of lambs with scented breaths.

Those that breathe your air, polluting it with the sick exhalations from their putrid entrails.

Wolves are not the real wolves.

The real wolves are those, behind colourful facades and clean clothes, defecating and urinating in the place where they lie, and living among their own excrement.

Those that know not how to tread on the right side of their hearts.

When I said: turn left, they turned right.

When I said: now to the right, they turned left.

When I said: look forward, they turned back.

Unlike you and your enlightened hearts that will never vacillate and will always know the right side.

He continued:

All the chosen ones will know when the time is right,

They will know it through Me when I speak in dreams.

Through Him that I called the Messenger.

And the crow will caw at the time of fate.

Get ready for the forthcoming battle.

It is I who made you.

And I did not look back.

And you will not look back.

Be under no illusion as you follow the path.

There is no left and no right.

The choice is already made.

He said finally:

I await you in my kingdom.

For you will always be My chosen army.
And what is Mine is yours and belongs to you.

That was what *He* said in the dream. *He* is among us.

For a few long seconds, there was not a sound.

Then in a jubilant cry, the gathered congregation called out *His* name.

The breath coming out of euphoric mouths, the nurturing syllables of *His* name, blew vertiginously through the basement. It was the big word that needed no questions, and no answers. The big word blew like the wind. It ruffled people's hair. Redheads, blacks, brunettes, blondes, whites. It stroked bald heads. The candles, which had stopped burning, as if they had suffered a sudden cardiac arrest, started burning again, reanimated. Once again there were shadows on the walls. On the euphoric faces. Eyes lifted to reveal nervous light. The believing eyes cried.

The men, the women, reinvigorated by this wind, raised their arms, their legs.

Heartbeats drumming in their heads, they made their way towards the altar.

Among the crowd with throbbing heads: the Prostitute, the Worker, the Maid.

The Messenger put out his warty hands. And from those ugly hands they received not the body of the Holy Host, nor the cup of the Holy Blood, but sheets of paper filled with scribbles, maps, floorplans, schedules, arrows and precise instructions for the plan that, at *the right moment*, would unlock the magic box.

A box decorated with the red ribbons of redemption, and the golden paper of eternal paradise.

Deep down, the promised gift of faith.

Gymnopédie I

The Implosion: A brief summary of the Bald Minister's most important sayings

The destruction of churches is another decisive step towards the creation of an efficient social state. *The Church's kingdom is not of this world.* So, if it does not belong in this world, it should not be built in this world. It is about growing roots. Faith does not spring from a building, nor does it spread through architecture. It makes no sense to needlessly occupy square metres of public space with such metaphysical excuses. Square metres that, used rationally, could be more profitably employed in other ways. Because, if indeed there is such a thing as faith, and if it persists in the face of adversity, then let God and his heavenly host occupy only the body of those who believe in him. And not take up public space. The house of God must only exist in the heads, hearts, hands, lungs, kidneys, penises, anuses and vaginas of those who believe in him. Beyond the flesh, God loses substance, ideas, emotions. It is pernicious, and a clear sign of disobedience, not to mention lofty arrogance, to establish metaphysical foundations outside of the only sacred temple, the only temple that can truly be recognised as a space for faith, which is the flesh of those who pray.

The time has come, then, to blow up all those tiled roofs and facades that claim to be divine.

The Director takes to the road

Cavernous morning.

Clouds hanging very close to the ground.

The Director takes to the road, pedalling like a metronome. His legs produce the steady movement that the bicycle requires. No more than that. The bicycle squeaks on the road that stretches out from the Wall and towards the Forest. The front wheel wobbles. The snow groans under the weight of the wheels.

This is the music for a lonely road.

With a discontented heart, a swollen bladder and a mind in turmoil, the Director cycles with lowered eyelids. His forehead, wrinkled with worry. He does not look into the distance. He knows the landscape, the road; he is tired. He has memorised the snow, the curves, the bumps, the potholes. The subtle steering of the handlebars. And the creaking of the wheels. Every now and then, he opens his eyes only to see the cloud of steam coming out of his mouth: life made visible.

Behind the Director, beyond the Wall and the Government Tower, the Factory's two chimneys are also puffing out steam, like his lungs.

So, this is it: everything repeats itself; what is inside is echoed outside; what is above echoes what is below.

While the Director's legs obediently repeat the motions, his mind chews on big thoughts. Many things have happened in the past few days, unforeseen and viscous and nonsensical: life leaving behind its incomprehensible footprints. And the Director, overcome by amazement, does not know what to make of it.

The Director possesses countless qualities, but perhaps lacks the robustness of character that might allow him to withstand the blows of the unexpected.

Even so, the Director is making an effort, not to pedal, but to think.

He says:

I don't want these thoughts, I want others.

To no avail. Perhaps only the dash of a startled hare appearing out of nowhere or the flight of a frightened bird might stop his careening thoughts, allow him to concentrate. Especially because, not long from now, the Director will be interviewing the Messenger.

The Messenger appears to know what will happen today, tomorrow, the day after tomorrow, and beyond.

And, for the Director, this is terrifying.

Boots reveal a man

The front wheel reaches the fork in the road. To the right, the Hospital. To the left, the Prison.

Clinging to the handlebars, the Director's suede gloves steer the bicycle down the chosen path.

The brakes are worn out, so he balances by putting his boots on the ground. Snow has gathered around the gate.

Winter is slow and fosters slowness.

With every step, the number 48 on his soles is recorded in a glacial footprint.

The Director assesses the imprinted weight.

He says:

Yes, boots reveal a man. And a man is the weight he carries. And the larger and heavier he is, the more the earth – or in this case the snow – groans and suffers under the greatness.

He dismounts.

The gate opens with the metallic clang of its out-of-tune mechanism. The on-duty guard, lit cigarette in mouth, had seen the Director from inside the security booth and pressed the button.

Without looking at the face of the guard writing down his name and time of entry in a logbook, the Director walks across the Prison courtyard, gloves gripping the bicycle.

A horse so close to ugliness

Everyone calls him *the giant*.

The Director is 2.08 metres tall, weighs 109 kilos and wears suede gloves.

(The Director never forgets that he has hands; the suede gloves are a reminder.)

He is wearing a cream-coloured anorak, a high-collared woollen shirt and corduroy trousers with snap-fly fastenings.

None of the clothes he wears can have any buttons.

As he crosses the courtyard, he can hear gasps of hunger. The Director looks around. A horse, its neck curved, over by the firing squad wall, is rooting around in the snow for grass that is not there.

The Director stops, speaks to it:

You shouldn't be here. You are too beautiful to be this close to the ugliness.

The horse is alive, it has light in its eyes, blood courses through its muscles. The wall is dead, it is a hard pillow for the bullets that pierce skulls and silence hearts: it is grey. The Director knows this only too well. He knows better than most what secrets the wall keeps. He steers the handlebar into a slight curve. The horse, still searching, its mane and tail fending off the cold, continues snorting at the whiteness hoping to find some greenery. As he approaches, the horse neighs. The Director stops. He groans. A sharp pain in the lower abdomen. The urine gathered in his bladder is beginning to show signs of impertinence.

He says to the horse:

The most important thing is to piss.

Persuasion Suite with chair upholstered in purple velvet

Third floor of the Prison.

Guards pass each other in a windowless side corridor. They whisper. One of them smokes. Smoke curls up towards the ceiling. Like fog. It mists up the ceiling light.

There are four metal doors in the corridor.

The number 48 boots stop in front of a door with a plaque that says: Persuasion Suite.

Besides the door: a button.

The Director presses: the door clicks open.

Green walls.

Four green walls line a space that is eighteen paces deep, nine paces wide. Three skeletal chairs face a desk. Behind the desk, a chair upholstered in purple velvet. On the desktop: a phone, books, papers, an intercom. In the corner is a metal bookcase with five shelves. Four of the shelves are filled with numbered dossiers. On the top shelf, a silent radio and a fish tank with some goldfish. A frame, one metre square, hangs on the wall furthest from the desk above the door leading to the adjoining room. In the frame, embroidered, the Government star on a blue background. Concrete floor and wooden skirting boards. A faint smell of pine trees. Cold air, seemingly insect-free.

The Director sits on the upholstered chair, his left eye flickering. Last night he got out of bed six times but was hardly able to piss. Thirteen drops. He kept count. Six times for thirteen drops. Pathetic. His right leg trembles. He feels an itch. Eczema on hidden skin. The itch makes him anxious. And anxiety increases the itch. The itch is a larva born of anxiety.

He gets up. The kneecaps creak. He takes off his anorak and puts it onto a clothes hanger. He uses only three fingers for the task. His pinkie and thumb remain immobile beneath the suede.

He scratches his belly. He strokes his beard of many years. He is proud of it. The beard makes him appear fearsome. It hides most of his sincerity, and his weakness. Hidden behind a rough beard, the Director only reveals what he must.

He sits down again.

With elbows on the desktop, hands holding his jowls, he reads a case file. Without taking his eyes off the paper, moving like a building crane, he lowers his arm and presses the intercom button.

A gruff voice asks if he needs anything.

He replies:

No.

And then, he orders:

Don't let anyone in.

From a hidden pocket he fishes out a small box. He uses his teeth to pull off one of his gloves. His hand now uncovered, he uses the nail of the ring finger to flick open the top. He puts a pink-coloured tablet onto his tongue. He sinks back into the velvet.

He feels the chemicals melting. Absorption taking place.

The Director's organs respond obediently to the chemical onslaught. Mostly his heart. The Director's heart rate slackens, slow as a cloud. And with a slower heart the Director's head is steadier, ready for the battle to come: the interview.

The Director puts the glove back on and redirects his attention.

The case file is numbered: 1748.

Gymnopédie II

The Fear: A brief summary of the Bald Minister's most important sayings

A Government that wishes to rule with courage and seriousness must assert its control through fear.

Before money, or hunger (hunger is the stomach's fear), or the homeland, or the flag, there already was a *bogeyman*. Like a contagious virus. Few know its origin. But it was already there in the amniotic fluid, that is a fact.

Fear, therefore, is the largest surface on the human relief map. In the hierarchy of human feelings, it takes up as much space as skin does in the hierarchy of human organs.

Fear and skin: long-time neighbours that greet each other cordially when they meet.

One starts when the other starts; one finishes when the other finishes.

The executioners talk (I): To make our hackles rise

In the corridor's stagnant cold, the three men appear to be smoking with each breath despite having no cigarettes.

Two executioners hold a handcuffed man by his bony arms. This pale and filth-covered man, dressed in an orange jumpsuit, is the one everyone calls the Messenger.

One of the executioners has a glass eye. And a single eyebrow: bushy. A hairy caterpillar that makes the eye sockets look disproportionate. The dead eye does not see, so it does not cry. Instead, it pierces with fear and a flash whoever is seen by it.

The executioner alongside him looks straight ahead. His head is still. Not moving down, or up, or left, or right. Because of a problem with his spine, he needs to wear a neck brace.

Seen from the outside, the executioners look more like men being tortured, like men subjected to suffering, rather than men whose duty is to devise tortures to make others suffer.

Callused knuckles. Fingers punished by metal. Repeatedly. Glass Eye watches the cuffed hands. The heavy door budges. It sings a high note as it opens. A fast smile flashes on the Messenger's mouth. A ringed left hand pushes on the polished door handle.

The Messenger is the first man. He sits facing the desk at which the Director's head lingers over some paragraphs in the case file. The two executioners remain in the room after uncuffing him. They each pick up a skeletal chair and move to the back of the room. There, they sit beneath the frame in which the star of the law gleams.

Glass Eye pulls out a pack of cigarettes. Takes one. Holds it between his teeth. Strikes up the lighter. His dried-up lungs rattle with a cough. He stretches his arm out and offers the other man a cigarette. Neck Brace goes through the same motions. Though he does not move his neck, or cough.

The executioners stretch their legs and push their backs against the wall as they smoke. They must save their hate for later. They focus on the lit-up stage. As if in a theatre, before the start of the show, they exchange views in low voices.

Wanna hear something?

Sure.

Yesterday I got home, and my wife asked me what I thought of her ass.

And what did you say?

Nothing. I grabbed her and pulled her into the bedroom for a closer inspection. The children were having their soup. I locked the door. I made her lie down on my lap. Her ass towards the ceiling. I lifted her skirt. I pulled down her knickers and I gave her a good spanking.

What did she do?

She was crying.

And then?

She was calling me names: one-eyed bastard, one-eyed bastard, she kept shouting. It was the only thing she could say.

And what did you do?

I spanked her some more.

And then?

Whadya think?

You screwed.

That's right.

And you never answered her question.

Of course not.

Deep down, that's what it was all about . . .

That's right.

Women only tell us what they really want when they're getting a good beating. I'll never understand them.

That's what they're there for.

To get a beating.

To annoy us.

That's right.

Glass Eye takes a deep drag of his cigarette. With smoke coming out of his mouth, he says:

I really needed that . . .

Hitting her?

No, I mean having a smoke. Shame about these chairs.

The giant has the right idea.

Purple velvet. Now that is comfort: like a king sitting on a cloud . . .

And have you seen the fish tank?

Huh . . .

Today it only has five fish. There were six last week.

Who knows, he might be having them for dinner.

Quiet . . . They're starting . . . Do you think the Messenger will get away?

This bastard? Surely not.

The executioners tuck their legs in. Bend their knees. They extinguish their cigarettes on the bottoms of the chairs and put the roaches in their pockets. They put on their best church manners and faces.

Glass Eye coughs. Pulls out a handkerchief. Spits into it. Examines it closely.

Interview with the Messenger (I):
On wanting to stitch up orifices

The Director lifts his eyes from the case file when he hears the cough at the back of the room. On the front of the orange uniform is a tag with the number 1748. The Director examines the Messenger's face with its beaked nose. Then, he scrutinises the hands.

The Director notices the evidence: minuscule fleshy flowers are sprouting from the other man's fingers. Warts.

The Messenger, sitting in the uncomfortable chair, hands intertwined, gazes at the fish tank. The Director says a name. The Messenger turns to face him. In a friendly tone, the Director asks four questions about the wolf attacks in the Forest. His words are sugar-coated, like sweets. The Messenger, a diabetic, refuses to answer all four times. Grimacing and baring his gums. So the Director repeats his questions. And the Messenger repeats his silences, now brusquer.

The Director tightens his jaw. He grinds his teeth and gets up. The Messenger's gaze follows him. He notices how the Director's reddened ears, seemingly detached from his head, move as he moves his jaws. He also notices the small shadow projected against the green wall and he frowns.

He thinks:

The Director's shadow does not match his size. He's a giant . . . But the shadow attached to him is like a dwarf's.

The Director moves towards the shelves. Out of the corner of his eye he sees the seated executioners. He turns on the radio. The Government's station is broadcasting a piano sonata. The sonata detaches itself from the radio. It bounces off the walls. It picks up the pace to a furious gallop. The Director bides his time, arms outstretched, gloves parallel to his pockets. He dips his gloved finger, like bait, into the fish tank. Observes the predatory dance. Draws on the water's skin. The five fish jostle to reach the suede ahead of each other.

With the sonata holding him aloft, the Director starts:

This. Listen to this. It's . . . Can you believe the beauty? When I hear it – and I've heard it countless times, you know? – it makes me want to stitch up all the orifices in my head. Yes. So the chords won't fly away and will remain in here for ever. Here, screaming inside my head. Hearing this can save and cure. Can you believe the beauty? Just listen to this progression, this pure mass of strings . . . It's like I say: it opens new possibilities. It almost makes the heart skip a beat . . .

The Director takes his gloved pinkie out of the fish tank. The fish open and close their mouths, releasing bubbles. And, retracing his steps, with the gestures and intensity of a remote-control doll, the Director sits down again on the purple velvet seat.

Gloves on his lap:

The heart almost skips a beat. It almost changes its rhythm. Don't you agree? Do you not like this sonata? Or don't you believe in music?

The Messenger ignores the provocation: he is busy removing dirt from under his fingernails. The Director observes him, continues:

You can say it. It's perfectly natural. To not like it, or not believe in it. But this is true: persuasion, like music, is an art. And art needs an artist to hold onto emotion and an object that deserves attention. You don't agree? Of course you do. You know it well enough. Of course you do. You are also a persuader. Deep down we are all persuaders trying, at every turn, to persuade better, aren't we? To persuade ourselves, and others. To persuade with a plan. So that our egos, with sharpened beaks, can draw blood in a cockfight. And win, of course. I'll be honest with you: I don't want to fight you. I'm not a cockerel. But if you refuse to cooperate . . . if you persist in your stubborn pride, you'll make my job harder. I'll tell you something else: I don't care if you had a dream about the attack in the Forest or not; if you have premonitions or fortune-telling skills; if God whispers the future into your ear at night; if you're lying or telling the truth. That's right! I don't care if you're lying or telling the truth. Don't believe me? It's hard, I know, but I don't believe there are any honest men. For me, and I must stress, for me in particular – and you may find this strange – it's not events that matter. I'm interested in the whys. I'm giving you a chance to answer questions about the whys. You know, many people would give everything they have, and even what they don't have, to talk about the whys, even if they don't have the answers, if only to be heard by others, and therefore to hear themselves. That's what saves them from being alone. Being able to say: I want you to listen to me. So now I am here, in front of you, listening.

With the sonata playing in the background, the Messenger cracks the knuckles on his wart-ridden fingers.

The Director shifts uncomfortably in his chair. Excitement makes him want to piss.

After a pause, having confirmed that he was right to be worried about this interview, he nods to the executioners, gets up and leaves the room.

The urinary question

Standing in front of the urinal, wearing gloves, the Director takes his penis between his index and middle fingers as if it were a cigar. He waits anxiously for the gush. He doesn't want a drip, he wants a gush of urine worthy of that name.

Drops of sweat, like rain, slide down the wrinkles on his forehead and neck. A nervous tic of his left eyelid makes him blink like a fluttering butterfly.

The Director's left eye opens and shuts in front of the tiled landscape. The nervous tic adds further anxiety to his wait. The stream of piss fails to arrive.

For the Director, over the past few weeks, this simple act – urinating – has become a form of torture: another needle in his daily life. The old pleasure has given way to sand-like discomfort.

In a tumult of muscles, the Director tightens his buttocks. He strains. He squeezes. The eyelash flutters its wings again. The acrid smell of bleach stings in his nostrils. Corrupts his sense of smell. The Director turns his nose away. Turns his head and his eyes to one side. Luckily the other four urinals are free of proud men with proud penises.

The Director sighs.

This way, at least, he is free of any added pressure, of having to urinate *as much* or as quickly as other men commonly would.

He was getting ready to tuck his penis back into his trouser fly when the Lame Soldier, rifle slung over his shoulder, came in to relieve himself. The Director recognises him. This is the cripple who, to everyone's misfortune, brought the Messenger into the Prison.

The polished boots move quickly, black and out of sync, out-shining the gleam of the tiled floor. The Lame Soldier hurriedly approaches the urinal next to the Director's. He could have chosen any other, but did not.

The two men, side by side, at the starting line, prepared for micturition, avoid exchanging glances. Or words. As might be expected. There is always some gentle embarrassment when sharing space at a urinal. Despite the male eye's temptation to compare sizes, the Director remained stock-still while the Lame Soldier prepared himself.

Immediately there was a gushing sound. Urine singing. Uninterrupted. Alongside a guttural *aaaaaarghh*.

Upon hearing that noise of sincere relief, the Director's prominent cheekbones take on the tinge of ripe apples. Rage pumps blood into his temples and arteries. And his penis, still inert, caught between gloved fingers, shrivels with shame and envy.

The Lame Soldier says:

I've been holding it in. That feels good.

Without turning his head, the Director grunts and nods.

The Lame Soldier's boots creak. Like hinges on a door. The Director's teeth grind.

The Director bows his head. He tends to his shrunken penis. He shakes the inert thing about, hoping it will resuscitate. Nothing. The ceramic urinal, attached to the wall, gaping, expectant, looks at him. It appears to be laughing at his poor urinary capacity.

The Director lowers his eyelids: the nervous one and the obedient one. And he concentrates. If that cripple could do it, so can I. He shuts his eyes to converse with what cannot be seen. The voice in his brain implores his bodily flesh for mercy. As if his flesh were an all-hearing God that is benevolent to those who obey its law.

Using the voice in his brain, the Director pleads:

Please, let me piss.

He immediately realises how absurd his request is. But despair leads to senselessness. Who really knows the flesh, the body? Who rules over the flesh, over the body?

It was not the Director ruling over his brain. Nor was the brain ruling over his unruly organs. In matters of the flesh, the soul has no say. If the soul were in charge, we would be immortal. But that's not how it works, the brain only gets complaints from the flesh, and issues the invoice. We pay the bills.

Tears of despair gather, in solidarity, in the Director's eyes. And from his urethra, stinging and weighted with pain, drip five drops of nut-brown liquid.

Interview with the Messenger (II): When cells refuse to hear

Once again sitting on the purple velvet chair, more on edge than he was before, the Director continues with the interview. The Messenger shows no sign of being unsettled by his return, quite the opposite: he picks distractedly at his fingernails and stares at the fish tank, spellbound.

Fine . . . I get it! I can see you don't like music . . . That's it, am I right? . . . Fine. Not even this admirable sonata. I respect your opinion. I honestly respect it, even though I can't help feeling sad about it. It saddens me. Now tell me, what's the point of me being here saying: this is beauty? Or: this is the closest we'll ever be to finding ourselves alone, in an empty room, looking at the eternity we've been promised! Do you get that? Or don't you? Of course you don't. Want to know why? Because something is getting in the way. A biological impediment. A microbe, if you will. It's true. And what use is it to force you, if your cells aren't disposed to move in that direction? Or are too lazy to get you there? What can I do? If the confused network of brain synapses, and the complex weave of nervous paths, or your arteries, reject the emotion and the beauty of music? Get it? Good. But they will, perhaps, allow beauty from other sources: divine, maybe? And who am I to declare that the many chemical reactions and electric currents happening in your body are wrong? Or that my body and my mind are right? Do you understand? To like music, or to not like it, is the end product of long and confusing chemical and biological processes. And it doesn't depend only on an education system.

The Director's lips move, hidden behind the beard and moustache, in aid of persuasion:

Listen to what I'm telling you . . . Pay attention . . . The true education . . . The only democracy . . . lies in not accepting biochemical differences; amino acid sequences; the molecular weight of proteins. I could force you to listen to the great pieces of music, like this sonata, all winter . . . I could . . . if I wanted to . . . but what would we have learned at the end of that process, what would the outcome be? Perhaps a tumorous growth, or perhaps you'd end up detesting the piano *glissandos* even more . . . Or maybe, you'd accept the combination of sounds, but in a phoney and artificial way. You'd accept the music through the force of habit. Through habit, even something we initially find abominable becomes tolerable, don't you agree? But that way you'd never be tapping into genuine emotion. The first and intuitive emotion, born of enzymatic reactions, opening up the heart. Even if I wanted to – and believe me, I do, and not only with you – I can't force you to be moved by music, just like you can't force me to believe in your dreams, your visions, or your God. Having said that, I hope you've understood what we are doing here. It's your turn. I want to hear from you. Hear the words you have to offer me. The whys. The causes. You can lie to me, if you wish. What I need are answers. Words to weigh and measure. Good words or bad. I need answers to complete the case file. That's what this interview is about. It's a bit of red tape, I know. Fortunately, or unfortunately, this is my job. And your job, at this moment, fortunately or unfortunately, up to you, is to answer.

*

The sonata rings in the ears once again as soon as the words give way to silence.

The Messenger scratches his lower lip, smiles. Cracks his knuckles. Massages his bruised cuff-free wrists. At the back of the room, Glass Eye dozes off with his mouth open: drool dripping. Neck Brace, sitting stiffly, notices it and nudges him with his elbow.

For the first time, the Messenger's voice, well articulated, with a slight accent, makes itself heard:

What are you hiding inside those gloves, Director?
Well! It's good to hear you ... You have a lovely voice ... But that's not an answer, that's a question.
Answer mine and I'll answer yours.
You're not understanding me ...
Answer mine and I'll answer yours.
What I expect from you are answers ...
Answer mine and I'll answer yours.
You're repeating yourself.
We're repeating ourselves.
Are you going to answer my questions?
I think some of those fingers aren't really yours, Director.

The utterance holds a knife between its teeth. The Director smooths his beard. One smile. Two smiles. The pent-up piss. The tremble in the leg. The butterfly in the eye.

The right-hand glove, resting on the crotch, moves suddenly. But half-way through its journey, it stops. Regretfully, it moves back next to its sister.

The Director warns:

You're barking up the wrong tree. You're in no position to negotiate.
I know some of those fingers aren't really yours. Yes, they're

prosthetic, Director. But I know even more. I know how you lost them. And how you can recover them . . .

Are you going to answer my questions?

I can tell you that I know many things you don't know. And if I tell you all those things that I know and you don't, you'll want to ask me more questions. Not the same ones. Others. Maybe those I can answer.

Now, you listen to me . . .

No, no, no. You're wrong, Director. You don't know what I know. You can't begin to imagine it. It's not in your case files. It hasn't happened yet. But it will happen, that's true. *He* told me. And, believe me, *He* is never wrong. And what I am keeping to myself is real news. An emotional time bomb. Not even music can overpower it. And then, for sure, your heart will skip a beat.

What are you talking about?

Do you really want to know?

Tell me.

Your wife will give it up.

What?

I'll say it again: your wife will give it up, just like that poor soldier gave it up to the wolves.

Give up what?

She'll give it up and she'll enjoy it, your Redhead.

The Director gets on his feet. Noise of boot soles. He turns off the radio. The sonata is interrupted. Some crystalline high notes still hover, for a second, clinging to the cold air, before being swallowed by the green walls' pores.

This is the cue for the executioners.

They get up, angrily. Step forward. No one knows the hatred they are capable of. They grab the Messenger by his bony shoulders. They punch him with closed fists. In the stomach. In the face. It is important to hit him in the face. They hit. That is where there will be marks that clothes cannot conceal, the shame, the hatred. They kick him. Knee him. There it is: all the rage contained in those muscles. The executioners are joyful as they hit him.

The Messenger falls on his knees, blood on his nose, in his mouth.

He shows defiance as he is dragged across the floor like a harmless dog. Still able to cry out some garbled phrases. Broken words, uttered by an exhausted mouth:

D . . . don . . . don . . . dontyou waaant to . . . knowww . . . how the Rrredheaddd will . . .

D . . . dontyou waaant . . . to knowww whaaat'll haaappen?

D . . . dd . . . on . . . dontyou knowww that . . .

How we need what is lost:
The sincerity of hands

The Director is an actor, stage front, following a precise script.

When he is standing, while interrogating or talking, he hides his lifeless hands, gloved in suede, behind his back. When he is sitting, it is easier: he places one glove over his crotch, then another, on top. And there they remain, immobile, the two furtive hands: useless twin sisters protecting one another.

As soon as he is alone, in his office, at his desk, behind a closed door, the Director pulls off his suede gloves. He uses the index, middle and ring fingers on both hands, assisted by his teeth. Six fingers for two hands. Three plus three plus his teeth. Which the Director uses to do the work of ten fingers. But having six fingers is not the same as having ten. And teeth cannot do the rest.

And what about the thumbs? How to compensate for the lack of thumbs? Humanity's development began with the thumb. What distinguishes humans from animals is the use of that dwarf digit, squat, opposable to others. Facing them, finger pad to finger pad, and counting, like a teacher counts the students he is about to teach:

One, two, three, four.

One, two, three, four.

*

Since *the loss*, there are some actions that the Director cannot perform: shake hands; peel a pear; fasten a button; turn a door-knob; shoot a revolver; touch a woman's skin in an arousing way.

Any manual action, no matter how small, brings some difficulty. It demands an additional effort. Constant attention. This, despite the tricks that his orphan fingers have forced him to learn.

But tragedy is also a place of learning.

Once, taking advantage of a personal invitation from the Bald Minister to deliver a theoretical lecture about *Persuasion Techniques* to recently graduated executioners, the Director wrote a manual.

The manual included a chapter called 'The sincerity of hands'.

At a certain point, it said:

. . . yes, it is true that almost everything can be seen in a person's face. In the head's facade. The signpost advertising what the heart keeps in store. There, in that collection of wrinkles, furrows, colours, hair, shadows, protrusions, orifices, is the key to the black box. The black box in which is hidden the dust of the human soul.

But the face has learned to lie. We do it from the time we are babies. With well-rehearsed and frequently repeated expressions. Applying the gymnastics of facial muscles.

Just like we are taught our ABC, there are techniques and remedies to help us control the raised eyebrows; the fluttering eyelashes; the smiling lips; the wrinkles of worry; or simply to narrow what we see.

To lie shamelessly with our facial expression and our inauthentic voice? Is that not something we all do once, twice, many times, and get away with?

So: where and how do we place our hands while our face and our voice are busy lying?

Inside our treacherous pockets?

Do we sit on them, claiming it is cold?
Do we hold one with the other so they inhibit each other?
Do we tug at tufts of hair?
Interlink our trembling fingers?
Scratch our heads?
Rub our noses?
Squeeze our earlobes?

How do we control incongruous gestures?
How do we control any action that is contrary to the words said and the expression conveyed?
That is the fundamental question.
Here is my advice: before any interrogation, release the suspect from his handcuffs, so that the hands can do the talking.

Hands occupy one of the top places in the hierarchy of language. And if we observe them closely enough, we will find the fault line. The lack of synchronicity. The delay. The hesitation. It is true that we are always too busy reading intent in someone's face, the twinkle in someone's eyes, or listening out for vocal inflections, or worried silences. But, to catch a lie, we must look elsewhere. Redirect our senses. Just like the tone of voice can tell us something about the speaker, hands, and their movements, if we are able to interpret them, bring us closer to the truth.

To lie simultaneously with body and soul, with both gestures and voice, is a difficult art. Only the great actors can do it and remain undetected. Serving up truth in the language of lies. Modulating the landscape of their voices in the territory of their souls. A symphony of hands playing the orchestra of the body.
In conclusion:
The face can lie through its seven orifices.

The voice can lie using words to serve its purpose.
Words can lie with every syllable.
But when we use our hands, the smallest of gestures can
betray us:
Hands can see in the dark.
They talk through movement.
They hear through touch.

A man of his word (I): Paying attention to the extremities

Beyond the Wall, in the Hospital, most of the halls and rooms reek of banality: ether, disease, death. In contrast, the Blond Doctor's office is perfumed with a mix of nail polish and acetone.

By the window, the Blond Doctor is filing his fingernails. From time to time, he looks out the window. A white blanket suffocates the Forest. The whiteness remains imprinted on his retina even after he turns away.

The quiet sound of fingernails being filed is interrupted by a female voice on the intercom. The Doctor does not respond. The right arm, suspended, bent at the elbow, continues its diagonal and rhythmic movements: forward, backward. As if, instead of a nail file, he was using a violin bow.

After filing his little fingernail, the Blond Doctor presses the button and says:

Send him in.

The Small Man came in. With hesitation, he climbed onto the patient's chair. Lifted one knee onto the seat and then the other. The Blond Doctor turned towards the wrinkled face. He pulled open the drawer. Put away the nail file. Sat on the green velvet chair. Extended his fingers, proudly.

Silence descended.

The Small Man did not know what to expect, or what to do. His feet swung nervously in the air, suspended twenty centimetres above the carpet. Amid the pent-up tension, his stomach rumbles. He seems to have a wild animal fighting within. He crumples his felt hat and repositions his bottom on the chair to muffle the sound. The Blond Doctor stretches his manicured hand towards the tray.

The Small Man takes notice, slides off the chair. He stands on tiptoes to reach the pot and pour the tea. The Blond Doctor observes his enormous head and his effortful plump hands. He bares his bright teeth as he sees the Small Man struggling in the face of the ordinary world.

Will you show me your hands?

What?

Your hands.

Why?

Just do it, come on. You'll pour the tea in a moment.

The Small Man, hesitant, walks around the desk. The Blond Doctor examines him.

See?

What?

Look carefully. Look. There. Now, look at mine. Do you see the difference?

Yours are bigger.

Wrong.

Your fingers are thinner and longer?

Don't be silly! It's not about size. And it isn't the fingers.

What is it, then?

Your fingernails. Look at your fingernails.

What about them?

Irregular. Grimy. Look at mine. Neatly filed. Ivory coloured. If you noticed the extremities, the tips of things, perhaps you might see the difference. But no, you are only interested in what goes into your mouth, in what you keep in your pockets, and in how you use your thingy with women who are twice your size. Unlike women, common men have a natural tendency to ignore the extremities. To neglect them. Fingernails, hair. Because they think: those things are not the *core* of my body, they don't matter. And yet, when we're in the grave, those are the things that persist. Much more than what is at the *core*. Women also resist and persist much more than men. Perhaps because they pay due attention to those extremities, and not only to what is at the *core*. And so: you show up here with an impeccable overcoat, a hat, tie, polished shoes, very well, but your fingernails, and your greasy hair, reveal the kind of man you are.

The Blond Doctor grips the Small Man's doll-like hands firmly. Watching him in distress, he releases them. He smiles.

Come, come, don't be scared. I'm not going to cut them off.

The Small Man sweats. Once again, the rumble of a stomach. He sips his tea nervously.

Take it slowly or you'll burn your tongue. Do you want a muffin?

No.

You sure? You don't know what you're missing . . . They're ginger, homemade.

Thank you. I'm fine.

Have you been eating lots of pies?

The Small Man looks down at the carpet, puts down his teacup and climbs onto the chair once again. His hat on his thighs.

A man of his word (II): Identifying weaknesses amid rumpled bedsheets

The Blond Doctor says:

Let me get to the point. I have some excellent news! I agreed the final details not long ago with the Bald Minister. Tomorrow, in the afternoon, there will be a Party meeting at the Government Tower. Followed by dinner. Then, the guests will visit the Club. Where you'll greet us all like the excellent host you are. Meanwhile, I hope you'll do something about those fingernails.

I'll try.

Have you chosen the girls?

Yes.

Who are they?

The Fat One, the Dwarf, the Bald Latex Queen, the Blind Girl, the Illusionist, and that bird, or rather that bloke, the one with the breasts and . . .

The one with a stiff surprise between the legs, right? It was me that put in those implants. The Bald Minister will love it. I'm very pleased with your selection.

The Small Man raises his upper lip in a loose smile.

The Blond Doctor laughs and claps like a child.

Pardon my excitement. I can hardly wait. All the colours of the rainbow gathered together. It'll be wonderful! I'd also like you to arrange some canapés. You never know . . . And some boys still smelling of breastmilk. Fresh meat. For the wives of some of our leaders, and who knows, maybe for our leaders themselves. Deep down, we all like playing, don't we? So, can you do it?

I'll try.

Don't try. Succeed. You'll be rewarded. You know I'm a man of my word.

I know.

So why the long face?

It's nothing.

You're unhappy?

No, it's not that . . . There may be something that . . . Yes . . . I mean . . . It may be a stupid thing . . . But . . . It's just that . . . I don't understand whose side you're on.

Me? Oh, my dear boy . . . You're worried about me?

The Blond Doctor puts down his teacup. He picks a muffin from the tray. He gets up. He walks around his desk. Sits on the desktop. Nibbles on the muffin. Gathers the crumbs in his mouth.

Do you mean do I lean to the left or to the right, is that it?

Yes.

Am I good or am I bad, is that it?

Yes.

Oh, dear boy, dear boy, dear boy . . . What matters least now is knowing which way the heart leans. Far more interesting, instead, to know where the heart will be in the end . . . Isn't it? Yours, mine. And what side will we be on? You don't know? I'll tell you. We'll be on the side of the winners. The battle hasn't even started and already you want to take sides? I have so much to teach you . . . To win in this world, all you have to do is appear to be prepared to help the weak in their revolt, while at the same time siding up to the powerful as they crush others. Because one of the two sides will win, right? In a dualistic world, they can't both lose.

We're playing with the wolves.

No, that's where you're wrong: we'll be lying down with them. Sleeping side by side with them. Fucking them. Is there a better place to understand the weakness of others than in their rumpled bedsheets?

It's risky. Rumours are already going round.

I love rumours. They're better than the truth.

Are you joking? This is serious. It's risky.

Come now, relax. Don't let yourself be influenced by loose tongues. You must learn to relax. Relax and adapt. The secret is in acceptance. There is a reason for everything. And there is no morality in nature. Just look at what she did to you! And I'll say it again: these days, whoever doesn't adapt, dies.

The Small Man looks down and starts running his fingers along the rim of his hat as if he were mending it.

A man of his word (III): A shame we don't have an exoskeleton

The Blond Doctor starts again:

That's right. Just think about rats and insects.
Rats . . .
Yes . . . Rats, insects, insects, rats. Although we should really aspire to be like insects. Yes, mostly them. It's a shame we don't have an exoskeleton. Just think: insects are everywhere. And in larger numbers. Why?
The Small Man does not reply.
They adapt. If one day this all ends, they will be among the few remaining creatures. And look at them: they may appear repugnant, fragile, insignificant. Easy to crush. But look at what a flea can do.
A flea?
Yes, just think of how many diseases it can pass on.
A flea?
My dear boy . . . Do you know what started the plague?
The Small Man does not know.
Just like in children's stories, it all started on a beautiful afternoon when a particular flea bit a particular rat. Later that night, the rat became ill. It was so ill that the other rats it lived with kicked him out. Over the following days, other ill rats bitten by other fleas came into contact with a man. As the rats died and the man watched them, the flea jumped off the rat and

bit the man. That night, the man became ill. The following day his wife kissed the sick man. And the flea jumped off the man, and then the woman became ill. And so on ... And do you know what the flea was doing amid the carnage? While humans and rats were dropping dead all around?

The Small Man opened his eyes.

It was copulating. Wait, I haven't finished yet, listen ... As you know, there were no insects or rats on Noah's Ark. But, after the heavens stopped pouring down, and as the waters began to recede ... Noah opened a window and released the crow.

The crow?

Yes, the crow. The crow went before the dove. The dove was Noah's second choice. So, the crow flew out and back ... And do you know what the crow found as it did its rounds, what it brought back in its beak when it returned?

Insects ...

Yes! And rats! To be more precise: rats, mosquitoes and praying mantises. Isn't that ironic? I mean, really ... These ginger muffins are delicious ... Are you sure you don't want to try one?

A man of his word (IV): Lots of people out there with longing in their teeth

The Small Man shakes his head. The Blond Doctor picks up a napkin. He cleans his fingers with care, dabs at the corners of his mouth. He looks around slowly. He furrows his brow and changes his tone: his voice darkens.

So how was the meeting with the Messenger?
  The meeting?
  Yes, the handover. Don't play the fool.
  Yes.
  Yes, what?
  It was in the Grey Zone's square.
  And?
  He was there with his boyfriend.
  What boyfriend?
  Yes . . . I think . . . I mean . . . I don't know if he was a boy-friend . . . It's what people are saying . . . A blond youth who also works with him at the Factory. A blond youth with a face covered in pimples. It hurts just to look at him . . . He has the face of an assassin . . . And so . . . He . . . They were there already . . . At the square . . . At the agreed time . . . On time . . . In the snow . . . I said good night and I handed over the suit-case. Wasn't that what you asked me to do?
  What did he do?

He thanked me, and said something about a crow that was going to caw . . . Sometime soon . . .

Well, how interesting.

He gave me shivers.

That's a bit much, don't you think?

Don't laugh. That man does not belong here.

Where does he belong?

Who knows. I don't. I only know that . . . Look . . . Look at what happens to me just remembering it.

The Small Man folds his jacket sleeve up to his elbow, unfastens the cuff button, and shows the Blond Doctor the goosebumps.

You can feel a presence. A light . . . A smell . . .

Of sulphur?

The Blond Doctor laughs again. From the mouth of the Small Man words are now flowing hurriedly:

Mock me, mock me all you want, you didn't talk to him, you don't know, you didn't hear him, when he speaks, he speaks our language, even if it's true that he has an accent, a strange accent. But he is something else, his language is something else, and he looked at me as he was speaking, except he wasn't looking at me, but through me, and he looked at me and, I don't know, it's as if he was seeing through my guts, through to the other side, and he could see on this other side there's something, that he could see, that he could see as if I were transparent, that thing I have on this side, he knows . . .

He knows?

Don't you hear what people are saying? He knows!

Please tell me, what are people saying?

Well . . . Since the wolf attack, it's all anyone talks about: the Messenger, and his visions, his premonitions, his dreams, and the devil knows what else! Don't ask me why. I just listen to what people are saying. He knows what will happen. He's married to *Lucifer* himself . . .

Terrific!

What do you mean?

People are very good at telling tall tales.

Tall tales? What about the dead soldier they found in the Forest? Hands, ears, eyes and feet chewed off? The wolves did exactly what he'd foreseen.

Listen: I have teeth and a stomach. You have teeth and a stomach. Hunger makes them hurt. There are lots of people out there with pain in their stomach and longing in their teeth.

What do you mean by that?

I'm not going to tell you everything I know.

What else do you know?

The Small Man's hands misshape the hat's brim.

The Messenger was arrested.

How?

This morning. The Bald Minister told me confidentially a short time ago. And all will be well, you'll see. He already has what he wanted, doesn't he? An army of loyal prostitutes and workers. The suitcase.

The Small Man trembles uncontrollably. He tries to string a sentence together but cannot: words come out of his mouth disconnected. The Blond Doctor gets up. He slaps the Small Man twice. The misshapen hat flies out of his hands. It lands by the polished shoes. The Blond Doctor opens the Small Man's mouth and forces him to swallow two brightly coloured tablets. Then he puts his arms around him. Pats him on the back.

Shhhhhhh . . . Now, now . . . Now, now . . . Calm down . . . A man your size shouldn't feel such big worries . . . I know . . . We're at a crossroads . . . I know . . . It's eat or be eaten. I promise you that those are the only two options for all of us, without exception. Even for the Bald Minister. You disagree? He can also see what's coming and he's nervous. He's very jittery. What do you think those dinners and parties are all for? To renew power of its energy, and to relieve it of its load. That's right! Were you expecting anything different? I've got them up to their eyeballs in tablets. But the drugs are no longer enough. Yes. They can sense it. The Government can sense it. They are beginning to smell the perfume of the incomprehensible. Just like you.

The Blond Doctor releases his embrace, holds the Small Man's face. He brings his mouth close to the oily forehead and kisses the furrowed brow. The wrinkles are squashed under the pressure of the kiss. He whispers:

I'm here, by your side. And all will be well, you'll see. You have my word. You know I'm a man of my word. That's why you and I do what we do.

The Blond Doctor moves his hand over the Small Man's thick nape, over the oily hair. He lowers his hand down to the crotch. He kisses the Small Man. After letting go of his tongue, he slaps him and squeezes his cock.

That's half a kilo you're packing! Fucking hell! It blows my mind. But for someone your size, your mouth reeks like a giant's. You're letting out farts left, right and centre. And those fingernails . . . Your half kilo of meat is rotten . . . rotten . . . Filthy. I'd suck your prick if I knew you bathed regularly . . . But you don't . . . That's half a kilo of shit . . . Go on! Get out! And take the tablet boxes for those swaps! And listen carefully! Listen very carefully: be careful when you meet the Director! He's always suspicious and may start asking questions. And if he does ask questions, don't answer them. None of them! And tomorrow: I want you ready, clean and washed! Don't fuck with me! Don't mess things up! Because if you do . . . If you do . . . You know I am a man of my word.

*

Cupping his nether region, the Small Man slides off the chair. He picks up the crumpled hat. Picks up the bag with the tablets. He asks, his lips weak:

And the Redhead?

The Blond Doctor, once again sitting on the green velvet chair, spreads the fingers of his left hand like a peacock spreads its tail feathers. The fingers reveal themselves one at a time. With the nail of his index finger, he points to the centre of his left palm.

The Redhead? The Redhead is here.

Gymnopédie III

The Meat: A brief summary of the Bald Minister's most important sayings

Of course, meat. The meat. How we need the meat.

Just look at the backward thinking that the people constantly repeat. I have on my table: cereals, pulses, vegetables. Countless nutritional possibilities, but even so people still say: I'm hungry. Hungry? Why? Because in the past a cut of beef would bleed on the plate at every meal? And what did this all lead to? I eat meat, therefore I can? I meat, therefore I am? Every day?

Does no one understand this? It is one thing to lack something, and quite another to feel plain hunger. To lack meat is not the same as to feel famished. Someone famished will steal, beat and kill. Someone lacking something will concentrate on what there actually is. On what is sufficient. And no one in this City can say, without lying through all the teeth stuck in their gums, that they are hungry. It is undignified! It is infamy!

As a Minister in this Government, I consider a slight shortage to be a necessity. A minor shortage should be mandatory for the people. Because it brings the people closer to humility, which is the right place to be. It makes them aware of what is necessary for basic survival. Without squandering, or waste. This much is true: whoever knows how to live only on what is necessary is truly rich.

The executioner's refrain

In the room next to the Persuasion Suite, after a bucketful of ice-cold water to shake his senses awake, the executioners force the Messenger to take off his orange jumpsuit, undershirt, pants, socks, shoes.

Nude and battered, the Messenger seemed to be famished.

On his nude torso, the recesses between his ribs are on display: a bone harmonium. Legs and arms, pitifully thin.

The Messenger puts his hands over his groin to cover his genitals.

Glass Eye strikes him with a truncheon:

Hands off, wart-man!

The executioners laugh like mindless chickens as they see the size of the Messenger's penis. Neck Brace winces in pain from the laughter and puts his hand to his neck:

Fuck me! That made me laugh so hard it hurt . . .

After they are done making fun of him, the executioners invite the Messenger to lie down on the iron bed bolted to the floor in the middle of the room. They extend the invitation by deploying the gentle hardness of their truncheons. They cover his torso and his legs with welts. They spit on him. The Messenger offers no resistance: he allows himself to be invited. He puts his hands over his head, lets them beat him. Tastes blood on his tongue.

*

Lying on the bed, the Messenger fixes his gaze on the ceiling. He seeks out a crack or a lump in its whitewashed texture. Something to distract him. To fix his eyes on something else and to feel less. He notices a spider weaving its web next to the bare lightbulb. Suddenly, the spider interrupts its weaving, hangs unhurriedly off its silken web, swaying from its thread like a mountaineer, its eight eyes simultaneously observing in close-up the Messenger's battered face.

The executioners secure the Messenger's ankles and wrists with the iron hoops attached to the bed. Beneath the bed is a mechanism of cogs and belts that makes the hoops move in opposite directions: wrists to the east, ankles to the west.

After the hoops have been adjusted and tightened around his tarsals and carpals, Glass Eye activates the bed's mechanism.

He sings:
  Stretch until he breaks.
  Stretch until he cracks.
  Stretch until he sings.
  Stretch until he splits.

Cacophony of torture

Snow falling: outside, over the Forest, over the Wall, over the City. And cold.

More cold outdoors than indoors.

But indoors, despite the cold, the Messenger is sweating from the pain.

Pain, like pleasure, reveals a sudden summer even in the middle of winter. It creates a fever, it gives off heat, it brings sweat to a body that was shivering earlier.

The screams buzz around the room like the sudden arrival of a swarm of bees.

The Director, who had earlier left the room for yet another unsuccessful attempt at urination, comes close to the iron bed.

A new pink-coloured tablet under his tongue: his heart tamed.

He observes the Messenger's gaping mouth: trembling; breath begging; teeth grinding; saliva pirouetting; and suddenly: a glimpse of the dancing glottis.

He sees the burning bush within the irises. The glaucoma of fear eclipsing the cornea.

He takes two steps back.

Hands possessed, disjointed.

The shouting of bones.

The Director watches closely, and in that spectacle he foresees a birth with the composure and calmness of an experienced obstetrician. It is clear: beneath that stretched-out skin, God is moving out and another body is being birthed, possessed by a different entity, orphaned of a master, of a father. On that iron bed another man is being born. A new man addressing the question of what-is-it-all-for-anyway? Because, when God moves out, men have nothing but themselves, their pain.

On the iron bed, the hoops stretch out muscles, bones, joints, nerves. The tonic scale of shouts goes higher as the cogs and wheels of torture make the Messenger grow by the centimetres he lacked in his adolescence.

As he observes *that birth*, the Director admits:

Yes, there is nothing but pain there. There is no man. Pain is always so honest.

Neck Brace asks:

Can we stop?

Glass Eye chants:

Stretch until he sings.

The Director glances at the hour marks on the white dial of his wristwatch, slides his tongue along the edge of his teeth, thinks about the Redhead, and says:

Just a few more seconds . . .

Ten dark seconds in one man's head, in another man's flesh

Just a few more seconds, the Director says again.

While the lazy second hand moved around the white dial, the Director pictured the woman, the Redhead, spreading her legs for the Messenger. And then for another man. He pictured men, standing in a queue, ready to lie on top of the Redhead. Working on her like worker bees in a hive. And the Redhead with her mouth creased, eyes rolled back, a queen bee, getting fattened off the men. Viscous liquid dripping between her thighs. Oily honey. Sullying the floor and the sheets with that oily honey. The Director pictured men drenched in the rain of fornication licking that honey off the floor and the bedsheets. Pulling their pants up. Calling out obscenities.

Yes, on the white dial, ten dark seconds for the Messenger, for the Director. But neither in the one man's flesh nor in the other man's head did they feel like seconds, nor did they feel like ten. Pain cannot be measured in time, and it cannot be communicated. Those two had not suffered in sync with the watch. Had they suffered, perhaps, in some other time, from some other pain, located elsewhere: in eternity? Nor was the strength of the pain in proportion to the distance travelled by the second hand. Those dark insignificant ten seconds hid thousands of hours of *private pain*.

Time and pain are not kind; they are unforgiving.

When they clash in one man's head or in another man's flesh, they do not look each other in the eye, they do not even shake hands in greeting.

To fall in love with a woman whose back was turned sixteen years earlier

A simple thing, and ironic: to fall in love with a woman whose back was turned and then be unable to flee. To be incapable of escaping beauty's hook.

But much patience and gazing at the moon are necessary when it comes to women: their bellies are always changing.

This is what the Director said to himself, for reassurance, when he thought about the Redhead.

The Director had fallen in love with the Redhead sixteen years earlier.

The Redhead was sitting with her back to the Director. Facing the organ in the church that had since been demolished. White skin, white dress, red hair, in stark contrast to the sombre light inside the Lord's house. An angel opposed to divine laws, fallen only nine days ago and already shorn of its wings, with a volcano erupting on her back. The dress, too brazen and revealing for a place of fear. One does not wear a white dress to mass. But that sartorial infringement gave the Director a shock in his stomach and a jolt in his groin.

After the lurch, the Director understood:

This one, with her back turned to me, is *the one*.

The one I want to gulp down until the glass is empty.

*

THE ARCHITECTURE OF FEAR

Beneath the half-lit frescoes of flagellated men with open wounds, smiling as they carried crosses on their backs, the Director used his hat to hide the bulge in his trousers, and made a decision that he continues to live by to this day . . .

Only weeks after first seeing her in church, when he invited her out for afternoon tea, starting the delicate task of wooing her, did he have the time and the proximity to examine the impossibly pale face in which everything seemed just right: the fine mouth, the aristocratic nose, even the dainty freckles dotting her cheeks like sprinkled cinnamon. He was also surprised by the unexpected power of her two-toned gaze: one eye green, the other brown.

It was true:

The Director had fallen in love sixteen years earlier. With a woman whose back was turned to him.

Thirteen years ago, he had married her.

Four years later, the Redhead's body expanded: their child was born.

And for the past two years the Redhead has not spread her legs for him.

The Director does the maths, he adds up and divides. He catalogues the bruises, the dark marks left on both the body and its affections, by those kicks delivered by time and marriage. And despite his calculations, every day the same thing happens . . . When he sees her in the kitchen, before kissing her good morning, the Director asks himself:

Who is *that woman* with hair the colour of lava and with mismatched eyes?

Who does she spread her legs for?

Why do I insist on loving someone I don't know?

When the amount is worthy of envy

Glass Eye's hand sought out the button. The machinery sighed. Machines also become tired.

The Director brought his bearded face close to the source from which the shouting gushed. Through his harelip, the Director blew into the Messenger's ear:

Hushhhhhhh.

In response to the sonic stimulation, steaming urine began rushing down from the iron bed and onto the floor, darkening the linoleum.

The executioners stepped away to avoid getting their boots wet.

They snorted:

Bloody bedwetter!

The Director, surprised, moved away to observe more carefully the size of the puddle of urine and the pattern it was making. And the inevitable happened. That which happens whenever a part of us is weak and we see in others the strength we lack. The Director envied the Messenger. He envied that puddle of piss. He wanted to shout out, but did not: he kept the lament to himself:

Even this wretch, even this wretch can do it.

Brimming with rage, he asked the four questions he had formulated previously in the Persuasion Suite. This time with no sweetener. By way of answer: only groans, sweat, flatulence, panting breath. The Director ran a numb tongue over his teeth and nodded. The executioners understood and walked around the puddle.

Neck Brace put two fingers into the Messenger's nostrils and tugged at his upper jaw. Glass Eye clawed into the gum beneath the lower lip, pulled open the lower jaw and, pliers in hand, entered the kingdom of the Messenger's mouth.

After much tugging, the calcium pieces were dropped into the Director's gloved hands: unrooted, bloody.

He counted them:

One, two, three, four.

The Messenger had passed out with the second dental extraction, so did not hear the Director's seven words:

A fair exchange: four silences, four teeth.

A lesson for fingers

The silence in the study is interrupted. The music is intense and insists on prevailing over architecture. It crosses boundaries. Rips through walls. Climbs up the stairs. Glides down the corridors like an elegant skater. Then, after crossing the closed study door, enters the Director's ears, weaker in volume but still authentically itself.

The music comes from the Son's coordinated fingers: ten growing digits grappling with the keys. Chords, left hand. Melody, right hand. Like the sounds of happy copulation, notes fill the house's empty spaces, as if they were pieces of furniture.

The Son is tethered to the piano. He is eight years old, but he has the dark circles of a grown-up: two black smears around the eyes.

From his Father he inherited the harelip, the hurried eyes. From his Mother, the red hair, the freckles and the pallor.

Tethered to the piano by his wrists and ankles, like a patient tethered to the machine that keeps him alive, the Son perfects a four-beat time signature under his Mother's impatient shadow.

He is preparing, with his Mother's guidance, for the big summer recital.

The Redhead shakes her happy curls. Rifles through the sheet music. She keeps the beat with her slim, slippered foot.

One, two, three, four.

One, two, three, four.

The Redhead watches with hawk eyes the Son's spider-like fingers moving over the keyboard. She is attentive to the precision and agility of those fingers often considered the weakest: the fourth and fifth. The ring finger and the pinkie. And she is prepared to punish him when he makes mistakes.

The Director, locked away in his study, listens to the piano lesson and tortures himself. He can do nothing about it. Stop it. Object to it. The Director knows that the Son's buttocks will feel the lash of a belt when his fingers stumble on the keyboard like drunks stumble about on the streets. And he can do nothing about it. Defend his Son. Hug him. He cannot prevent the harsh education. He cannot face up to the Redhead to rationally discuss the downsides of discipline.

The Director is the Father, and not much of one. The Redhead is the Mother, and very much so. The Director is certain that, if there ever were a conversation between the Father and the Mother, his arguments would fail him and, perhaps worst of all, his courage would fail him: his Son's gift torments him, and the music born from that cold discipline is a terrifying beauty.

When he listens to his Son playing the piano, evil seems to disappear, excluded.

Music, that great mystery, does not only prevail over architecture, but also pierces men's hearts.

The Director imitates the movements of the Son's right hand. Desists.

In the Director's heart, the delight caused by the music is replaced by the arrival of a feeling somewhere between pride and envy.

The Director admits:

These aren't enough.

My Son has all his fingers.

And this is how we avoid tendonitis

The door to the living room creaks and the Cat comes in. The Redhead glances at it over her shoulder. She follows the proud prancing of its cotton paws. The mewed disdain. She purses her lips and shakes her head. Her ringlets saying no. The Cat ignores her. It curls up on the carpet, by the fireplace. It yawns, taunting her. Turns its belly towards the ceiling. Raises its back leg. Starts licking itself. The fire crackles.

The Mother is carrying the bowl in which the Son had been dipping his fingers. With every step she takes, the wooden floor groans. The Son's fingers, still in need of relief, are dripping. He looks at his wrinkled fingertips as they leave a pattern of drops across the floor. And he holds back the real tears. Summoned by his Mother's severity, but held back through the power of his pride.

The Mother returns.

Once again, she forces him to immerse his fingers.

The Son complains:

No, Mother. No more. It's too hot.
That's right. That's how it has to be.
It burns.
It will do you good. You'll see. That's how it has to be.
Ouch . . . Enough . . .
It'll do you good. You have to be strong. That's how we avoid tendonitis.

But . . . It hurts.

Don't be such a baby. If you get tendonitis, the pain will be worse. Much worse.

No, Mother, if it's meant to do me good, it shouldn't hurt.

It has to hurt. Do you remember last year, when you fell and scraped your knees?

Yes.

Do you remember how it stung when I disinfected your wounds?

I remember.

You had to bite into a towel, didn't you?

I did.

And didn't that do you good?

It did.

Didn't that stop an infection?

It did.

Mother won't lie to you: I know it hurts, but that's how we avoid tendonitis. Because if you get tendonitis one day, it'll be much worse. Trust me. So don't you forget this pain. Hold on to it. Hold on to it. Someday you may find it's useful, you'll see.

But . . .

They're ready.

The Cat half opens its eyes. It jabs the carpet with its front claws. The Mother puts down the bowl and pulls open a drawer. The Cat yawns at the monotony. The Mother pulls a dish towel out of the drawer, the fabric is coarse. The Cat claws away.

Sitting on the piano stool, the Son watches his Mother return with dangerous equanimity.

He extends his scalded and shrivelled fingers with a gesture of surrender.

The Mother wipes his fingers tenderly. Then she ties his ankles to the heavy wooden stool and his wrists to the grand piano's gigantic legs.

The rope is long enough to allow the movements required to play the keyboard and the pedals.

After tightening the knots, the Mother kisses the Son on his forehead.

The Cat mews.

The fingers are warmed up.

The piano is waiting.

The fire crackles.

The lesson can begin.

Something is rotten in the kingdom of affections

The Mother and the Father, the Redhead and the Director, mindful of appearances, kept up the daily ritual that made the marriage seem alive.

The Mother's rigid lips brushed the Father's thin lips. Their mouths came together without desire, obstructed by the beard and moustache, in a dry but dutiful kiss.

The time and place were agreed in advance.

It was the Director's job to initiate. It was the Redhead's to receive.

The gesture most revealing of the vulnerability and affection between two people is a longing kiss. Not fucking. That is why prostitutes never kiss. A sincere kiss can break spells, raise the dead. Because that is where music from the lips converges with the defibrillator of shared saliva, the jingle of tongues. And the union takes place. What was once private is revealed. Everything we have been hiding comes to our mouths.

This was not what was happening. It had been a long time since the Mother and the Father, the Redhead and the Director, had shared their saliva. Or even the words that lead to dialogue. Or the dialogue that leads to affection. They used only the mono-syllables that allowed them to carry on organising the tedium of daily life. Even so, they continued to perform their shrivelled, cynical kiss. Every day. At breakfast. Wreathed in the fumes from the pots and pans. In front of the busy Maid. In front of the Son with his sunken eyes.

The suede gloves were the first to enter the kitchen. The first to be seen as the door opened. The giant made his way. In the middle of the kitchen, he proffered a telegraphic *good morning*. The Cat, slumbering near the Maid's feet, yawned. The Maid stopped chopping vegetables, straightened her thick eyeglasses, and replied.

As soon as the Father stood in the middle of the kitchen, the Mother, seated until then, keeping a watchful eye on the stirring of the soup, on the spoon in the Son's mouth, would interrupt her duties and stand up, smoothing down her skirt. The Son, mouth half-open, would put the contents of his spoon back onto his plate. And await, with a mix of disgust and curiosity, the coming together of those two mouths.

The freckled hand with long nails, painted blue, touched up the dormant curls. The arranging of the hair was the sign to come forth. The Father came closer to the Mother, with the scent of lentil soup flaring his nostrils. The Mother closed her dissonant eyes – green eye, brown eye – pre-emptively, to avoid despising him before consummation. And waited. The Father, knowing well enough about her temporary blindness, cast the busy Maid's bottom a furtive glance, and immediately looked away.

Only half a second. All it took was half a second of displaying affection in public for the marriage to formally endure.

Instead of: in the beginning was the word.
    Replace with: in the beginning was the kiss.
    Or: the kiss as a sign of the beginning and the end.
    Fornication in between.

How to chop vegetables in delicate times

The Maid's irises widen behind the thick glasses.

Through the kitchen window she tries to make out the shape of the horse. She stretches her neck, looks at the clock. 2:17 pm. Yes, almost time. For the next fifteen minutes, her sick heart will beat even faster, a victim of anticipation. The Lame Soldier will go past the window, mounted on his horse. And the Maid is preparing a surprise for him.

She turns the oven off. Opens the oven door. The infernal breath, hot and sweet, makes her turn her head away. Using oven mitts, she takes four muffins off the rack and puts them onto the worktop. She tests the cakes with a toothpick. Her eyes are animated by the intoxicating aroma of ginger. Once she has taken the muffins out of the baking tins, she wraps them in cloth: her fingers tingling. She looks at the clock again. The window. She straightens her glasses, hoping that desire will triumph over short-sightedness.

Outside, the streetlamps are anticipating night-time: they are lit, even though it is only 2:20 pm. The weak afternoon light feels enclosed: the Wall is ever-present. During these winter months, days are not well defined, they are puppets whose strings are pulled by the season's long nights. Days are almost black. As if the sun had fallen backwards into a ditch. As if the clouds and the wind had pushed it away and snow had filled its mouth.

The sun takes months to rise.

The Maid looks away. On the worktop, expectant and mute: onions, potatoes, courgettes. The vegetables to be added to the cooked lentils. She picks up an onion. Peels off its brown skin. The Cat jumps off the refrigerator. The Maid's cold feet are thankful for the feline warmth. The Maid puts the onion on the chopping board. She picks up the knife, with images of the Lame Soldier on horseback in her head and her Mistress's voice ringing in her ears. Her Mistress's strident voice always rings in her ears before chopping the vegetables.

Some time ago, her Mistress had scolded her:

Just so you never forget, and so I don't have to repeat myself or beat you, this is what you have to remember: we are living in delicate times. And delicate times call for delicate acts and gestures. If at the chopping board, knife in hand, you respect the vegetables' life-giving properties and the vital orientation of their subterranean growth, then the energy, the minerals and the nutrients you will receive upon mastication (if you chew at least thirty times) will be tripled and fully absorbed. No loss, no waste. Chopping a carrot or an onion the wrong way can diminish the absorption of energy and nutrients. Basic nutrients and minimal energy, true; almost negligible energy, you might say; but when added up it will increase the chances of survival, enhance longevity. Do you realise how important and delicate the task is? Remember that before you wield the knife.

The Maid shakes her head to get rid of her Mistress's voice. She looks out the window. Nothing. Knife in hand. On the chopping board, the onion, nude. Following the advice to the letter, the Maid delivers a single, firm knife cut, respecting the vegetable. She cuts the onion lengthways while thinking about her Mistress. Then she delivers another blow to one of the halves, thinking about the Lame Soldier. But the blade slips and catches one of her fingers. The curled-up Cat lifts its head and meows a second before the cut. The word 'shit' was ready to jump out of her throat like a frog's tongue darting for a fly, but the Maid swallows it just in time. It's just another cut. The fourth in a fortnight. Either her eyeglasses are no longer working, or the Mistress had been right when she warned the Maid about her fatal inclination for misfortunes:

Be careful, your blood is too acidic. You are too accident-prone . . .

The Maid's variations

The Maid shakes her head. Looks at the clock, the window, the cloth wrapped around the warm muffins. She rushes out of the kitchen with blood dripping heavily from her finger. Worrying that the Lame Soldier and the horse might walk past in the meantime. Without her noticing, a drop of anxious blood escapes the wound and drips onto the tiled floor.

There is the sound of steps in the hallway, and the clicking of the medicine cabinet's latch.

The Cat interrupts its lazing. Stretches its legs. Perks up its ears. Meows. Walks towards the soiled tiles with its tail up. Sniffs. Then licks.

The cabinet clicks shut, announcing the Maid's return.

Breathless, the Maid comes back into the kitchen with a hand pressed tight against her wound. She sees the Cat licking the tiles. Kicks it away. The Cat is aggrieved, its hair standing on end. She breathes in. Once, twice. Catches her breath. Looks out the window. The Cat, recovered, approaches her, slowly. It purrs, needily. The Maid's fingers reach out to scratch the top of its head. Unexpectedly, or perhaps not, the tiny sandpapery tongue licks her wound. The Maid slaps him away and the Cat leaves the kitchen. From the pocket of her apron, she pulls out a jar of mercurochrome and a cotton ball. She dabs at her finger. From the same pocket she extracts a plaster and places it over her cut. She tightens the lilac-coloured apron. Takes five steps. Shuts the door.

Looking out the window, the Maid scans the road and sees no Lame Soldier and no horse. Shit, perhaps they've gone past already, she mutters to herself. She gets back to the kitchen counter. Tightens her fist. And she slams it three times against the tea towel covering the cakes. She smashes them. She bites into the cotton until it hurts. And she throws the tea towel and the smashed cakes into the rubbish bin.

Standing over the chopping board, she adjusts her eyeglasses nervously. Her cut hurts. She picks up the knife. She brings the dangerous blade close to her lenses. The smell of the onion's blood. Her pupils dilate. She hears music. The lesson has started. In the room next door, the little pianist's fingers strike the right keys with quick certainty and produce the miracle. The Maid can clearly make out the marriage of melodies. Chords heralding a march. The happy tempo. She has been hearing that piece for so many months and it still makes her emotional every time. Despite the Blond Doctor having warned her:

Do some light exercise: walking, cycling, but avoid strong emotions.

But how could she not become emotional listening to the piano every day? He has golden fingers, the Mistress's Son! Knife in hand, she mimics the movements of a conductor's baton, her gestures mirroring the Mistress's hand moving rigidly over the Son's shoulders.

Now she, the Maid, was the Maestra. And the vegetables were the colourful orchestra.

With virtuoso movements, the Maid's hand brings the sharp blade down on the onions, carrots, potatoes, courgettes. The knife, tuned in C minor, cuts an *allegro*. And the vegetables offer themselves to the sacrifice, they give in, from their skin to their pulp, they surrender to the chopping board, to the varieties of mutilation.

The blade delivers its blow.

The knife in mid-air. Synchronised with the pianist's hand as it hovers over the keyboard. Silence punctuated by the disorderly beating of a heart. The Maid lets the knife fall on the vegetable orchestra. She listens, her skin erupting into goosebumps. The second movement: *adagio*.

The melody travels down the corridor.

In an emotive gesture, pushing the chopping board to one side – some of the vegetables roll off – the Maid leans her torso and her bra-straitened breasts over the kitchen counter. Parallel elbows. Head hanging. Eyeglasses slipping down her nose. Buttocks protruding towards the closed kitchen door: a fragile wooden barrier that the music can easily breach, like an experienced burglar.

The music's invisible hand brushes the Maid's shoulder; it caresses her hair; follows the contour of her full hips; fondles her soft breasts; unties her apron strings; lifts her skirt; tugs at her knickers' elastic; and with its universal tongue licks the inside of her hard thighs. The Maid shakes her head to say no, but spreads her legs further.

The Maid cannot hold back tears as her clitoris tingles and her anus clenches. She falls onto the floor, faint. She touches the scar on her chest, a track printed onto the skin holding her racing heart in place.

She says to it:

Shhhh, don't be afraid, it's not him, it's not the gloves, it's only music: chords like hands.

Gymnopédie IV

The Music (I): A brief summary of the Bald Minister's most important sayings

Let us all agree: how dangerous it is to hear birds singing happy melodies. How dangerous it is! Fortunately, the Wall acts as a barrier, the Forest is far away, as are the tree canopies. But let us not be careless. Music is not merely, as many believe, the mathematical arrangement of sound. Or a question of 'how lovely!' Or of 'how horrible!' Music is also a remedy: it can have the innate efficacy of an anxiety drug or possess powerful tonic properties. It can change moods, alter heart rates. Like a high-calibre gun in someone's hand, a cello or a saxophone can knock down, immobilise, silence, soften, bring tears where there were none. And in the same way, as we all know, a piano can make our bodies slip, or jump up like a cricket, or send us running and grinning, propelled by gusts of joy.

Having said that, some inevitable questions arise:

What music should the Government listen to in order to make itself stronger, and more unbeatable?

And what music shall we play for the unsophisticated minds and the rudimentary hearts that abound in this City, so that rage does not foam in their mouths?

Without discipline there is no world

The Son's fingers, though immature, are definitely ripe for the task. They may lack the agility of a horse's gallop, or the grace of an octopus's waltzing tentacles, but, with intensive training, with much drilling, they will do well, the Redhead believes.

While she stitches the potatoes together, she says to the Son:

Your Mother will live past a hundred years. You know that, right?
Yes.
And why?
Because of the rice.
Yes, the rice, and what else?
Because of the vegetables and lentils . . .
Yes, all of that, and anything else?
There's something else?
There is.
Because you don't eat the meat pies . . .
True . . . But not only that.
I know: because you chew your food many times . . .
That's true. Thirty times for every mouthful. And . . . ?
I don't know.
Think hard.
I don't remember.
It's discipline, isn't it?
Of course, discipline.

Without discipline there is no world. With no world there is no music. I told you this before.

Yes.

You want to be a pianist, don't you?

I do.

You want it a lot?

A lot.

You know Mother loves you, don't you?

Yes.

And you know that Mother only wants the best for you, don't you?

Yes.

So that you'll be a great pianist and Mother will live past a hundred . . . With?

Discipline.

That's it. Mother does this to forewarn you.

What is that?

Forewarn?

Yes.

It means to tell you what will happen next.

Okay.

I don't want you to get distracted. If you stay close to the piano, you'll be protected. Someday you'll thank me, you'll see.

The strung-together potatoes

To perfect the Son's innate technique, there were also the potatoes.

The Redhead would string together two potatoes, skin and all. The potatoes were chosen by size. They had to fit within the palms of the small hands. The Redhead strung the potatoes together with a needle and thick thread. Repeatedly. She would then put the potatoes, strung together, into the Son's hands. And she would force him to grip them firmly.

The Son spent entire mornings unable to tighten his hands into fists. Or to use them for anything other than: potato hands, cupped hands, dead hands. Unable to play, he sat on a kitchen chair, swinging the potatoes up and down, like an improvised yoyo, half expecting that the repetitive movement might make one of the potatoes break loose. He handled them while distract-edly noticing the Cat's laziness, or observing the Maid doing her chores, but gravity had no effect, nor did the potatoes tumble to the ground.

And so, his piano-playing technique was being perfected.

Eyes blue like a deep river

The short-sighted Maid cycles slowly.

Sound of wheels and whistling wind.

The heart beating fast.

Breathless.

Snow, frozen muddied puddles on the pavement, tarmac, cobblestones.

Arriving at the square with the cafés with yellow awnings, in the Yellow Zone, the Maid slows down to catch her breath. She takes her feet off the pedals but does not dismount. She puts her heavy boots on the ground to keep her balance. She tries to calm the drumbeat of her heart, standing by the obelisk erected by the Government after the Great Disaster. The Maid likes the obelisk. It has an inscription carved into the stone. The Maid reads it but does not understand. *CAVE HOC ILLUDQUE.* It is written in a foreign language. Perhaps that is why she likes the obelisk. Not understanding is vast, it never ends.

She lifts her coat collar, fixes her hair, pushes her thick eyeglasses into place. Out of her handbag she takes out a muffin. Nibbles, chews, swallows. Looks skyward. The raised flag with the Government's star blows at the wind's whims. The moon blinks through the clouds. The Maid puts the bitten muffin back in her handbag. Steers the handlebar. She puts her heavy boots back on the pedals.

Heart beating fast in her carotids, chest heaving beneath her nightgown, she approaches the checkpoint around which barbed wire had been sown and had grown as vigorously as noxious weeds, overnight, without anyone noticing. A sudden rush of heat climbs from her belly to her face as she approaches the soldiers: imminent danger brings out a blush.

She stops near the barrier. Does not dismount.

Her frozen fingers produce a pass and hand it to a soldier. His eyes are blue like a deep river. He is smoking. The Blue-eyed Soldier blows out a couple of puffs. After checking the pass, he calls out. Another soldier, short, bald, with no beret, comes out of the glass booth. After a brief exchange of murmurs, the bald soldier returns to the booth and the one holding the stamped pass looks her over.

Anything wrong?
    I'm visiting a sick relative.
    Do you know what time it is?
    It's twelve past eleven.
    You know it's dangerous for a girl to be out in that Zone . . .
    I can take care of myself.
    I'm not saying you can't.
    I need to see a sick relative. Besides, this pass allows me to access all Zones, right?
    I'm just following protocol. You understand?
    I understand. But I have a sick relative I need to see.
    Yes, you said that already.
    The soldier's blue gaze moves over the Maid's body.
    Nice bicycle you've got there.
    It's just a bicycle.
    I used to have one like that. I'm just saying, it's a nice bicycle. Want a cigarette?
    I don't smoke.
    What time will you be back?
    I don't know. But I'm not having coffee with you.

I didn't ask you to have coffee with me.

I'm ahead of you.

The Blue-eyed Soldier smiles.

The short-sighted Maid feels a palpitation. Puts her hand on her chest. From her ungovernable heart a thin stream spills, making her wet. Her knickers damp.

Without taking his blue eyes off her thick frames, he bends over. He stubs his cigarette out in the snow. Puts the butt into his shirt pocket.

He points the barrel of his rifle towards her heart.

Are you aching there?

No.

You sure? I think it's beating hard because it likes me.

No!

No need to blush . . . What's the address?

Excuse me?

Your relative's address? Aren't you visiting someone?

23rd Street, apartment 408.

Very good.

Yes.

I'll be here when you return. In case you've changed your mind.

I don't change my mind.

Let's see . . . Who knows? Life's full of surprises.

Maybe.

Best wishes.

. . . ?

To your relative.

Oh, thanks.

And beware of the wolves.

Sorry?

The soldier winks an eye blue like a deep river, hands back the pass and raises the barrier.

The cowardly act of courage

That morning, by order of the Bald Minister, a group of soldiers had raided the Factory's north wing and dragged the Messenger, handcuffed, into the Prison.

In apartment 408, sitting on the edge of his mattress at the end of his shift, gun in hand, the Worker with the acne-covered face flicks open the revolver barrel. He inspects the bullet chambers. Presses his lips. Whistles. Fills the void with a melody.

Gently, at random, he inserts a bullet.

He closes the now pregnant barrel.

Spins it.

A grey moth flutters over the sweaty hands, barely avoiding the lampshade's green light. The cylinder's metallic spinning is as brief as the zig-zagging flight. The barrel stops as the moth lands on the wardrobe's mouldings. After he cocks the gun, seconds abound.

The Worker's hands tremble. A head gesture, a glance at the watch.

11:19 pm.

He says:

It's time.

The Worker opens his mouth. The barrel is cold against his tongue. Index finger on the trigger. Saliva gathering around his gums. Inside his underpants, the penis stirs. Telling him it wants to play. To gamble with death is arousing.

He says:

Now, to top myself.

He hears the finger's pointless effort:

Click. Click.

The Worker falls back onto the mattress with not a drop of blood. No hole in his skull, no grey matter splattered over the walls.

With the still-cold revolver in his hand, the Worker looks out the bedroom window at the City's clustered lights, now dimming under the smoke belched out by the Factory's chimneys.

The Worker swallows hard to hold back the vomit. His heart is beating in his gums. Laughter charges in, attached to nausea. The Worker drops the gun and pulls a pillow onto his face. Clenches his teeth. Sinks his head into the pillow. After the laughter come the tears: the liquid trace of his cowardly act of courage. Wet pillowcase.

There is a knock at the door.

The Worker wipes tears from his eyes, sniffs. Hides the revolver beneath the pillow. Gets up from the bed. Takes seven steps down the corridor. He peers through the door's peephole.

He sees a pair of small and faraway eyes behind thick glasses.

He opens the door.

Embraces his sister.

They took him away. Now who will speak the words?

A red X

After making sure she had turned the key twice, the short-sighted Maid removed her skirt, her wet knickers. She spread her thighs. Separated her trembling knees. Looked at her feet. Examined the ground. Small drops of blood marked the distance between her ankles. The Cat mews outside the bedroom, approaching. She put her hand to her dormant vagina. A hot and bright fluid glazed her fingertips: evidence of her recently demolished maidenhead. No, that was not period blood.

Her heart ached even more.

It beat hard, overflowing.

In the empty air, she could hear the machine-gun fire of her fear.

From the dresser drawer the Maid took out a hand towel, a sanitary pad, clean underwear. The Cat mews and scratches at the door, upset. I can't let you in, she whispers. She folded the hand towel until it was four fingers in width. She pressed the sanitary pad against herself, to prevent leakage, and used the towel to secure it, like a chastity belt. She put on her knickers. She lay down. The Cat gave up.

The flow would have to stop.

The heart would have to empty itself.

She pulled a calendar and a pencil case out of the hiding place beneath the mattress. Inside the pencil case were twelve coloured markers. The Maid chose the red marker and drew an X on the 23rd day of the month. She marked the day. She singled it out not only because it had passed, but because she had made a mistake. And mistakes have to be marked in red. Not wanting to forget it, to avoid repeating it later, she marked it.

The Maid was not only recording the mistake, but also the evil act.

The 23rd day would be remembered like this.

A red X in the calendar.

The shyness of sad things

Seventh day after the Messenger's arrest.
    The voice of snow is no longer heard across the City.
    The tarmac is soft. It muffles the tumult.
    The City's architecture wrapped in winter's coat.

In every street of the Brown Zone there are houses with male workers, female workers, child workers. Windows are lit. People are alive. Light comes from within the houses.

The Worker is walking down the pavement. He sees passers-by, tired shoes, tall horses. Weapons gleaming in military hands.
    The Worker hurries towards the Factory carrying a suitcase. Inside the suitcase are his uniform and his packed lunch. And, shortly, one other thing.
    Without anyone noticing, the Worker makes his way with hatred in his boots, and with faith in his heart: he tightens his fists, compresses his fingers, bites his lip until it hurts. The snow muffles the groaning of his footsteps. His boots sink deeper.

He has nurtured faith and hatred as if they were delicate flowers, watered regularly. They have grown hopeful roots in the red flowerpot that the Worker hides within his chest. And no one realises how dangerous it is to be hiding a flowerpot.
    At 19th Street, his woollen beanie on his head, the Worker picks up the pace to avoid being late. 19th Street, like 20th, 21st,

22nd and 23rd Streets, leads straight onto the Brown Zone's central square. Wherever he looks he sees white and brown. Snow lashes his acne-covered face. It lands on building facades.

After crossing the square towards the barbed-wire curtain, the Worker approaches the checkpoint: his left hand seeks out the stamped pass in his coat pocket. The pass is given the all-clear with bellicose eyes and lowered brows.

The barrier raised, the Worker's boots finally step onto the Grey Zone's muddy ground.

The Factory's sirens announce the change of shift. They have the precision and the inexplicable power of prayer. In this last part of his journey, the Worker walks with his right shoulder against the Wall. Built in the north of the City, the Factory runs up against the Wall like a shipwrecked cruise ship.

The Worker stops. Looks at his watch. Dark seconds. Looks back. No one. Through his nostrils, he inhales the knife-cold air. He spits, and his sputum lands on the Wall. The Worker watches it sliding down the concrete like a snail leaving a trail of slime until the cold paralyses it. He continues on his way.

Crusty snowflakes fall tirelessly from the sky.
The shyness of sad things.

Gymnopédie V

The Colours: A brief summary of the Bald Minister's most important sayings

As it is not possible to colour-code thoughts, to make them more orderly, this Government has opted for demarcating through urban development the many types of people that exist. And the smells they emanate. Once suitable colours are selected, and the precise boundaries are established, we can proceed to painting buildings and laying down barbed wire. Once this has been executed, we can move on to segregation: separating the herd, one head at a time. Populating each of these colour-coded Zones with the temperaments that seem most appropriate for each. So that, even from a distance, and before crossing the borders that restrict this urban rainbow, we know, for instance, that those living in the Blue Zone will possess the right qualities: order, clarity, discipline, stability. And, by contrast, the Brown Zone immediately alerts us to what it holds in store: dirtiness, incoherence, nausea, violence.

Symptoms and smells

The smell of death and the smell of pies mingle in that place, more than anywhere else in the City, in a strange and repugnant mix. The Worker looks up. The two chimneys – gun barrels pointed at God's realm – continue belching out endless clouds of smoke: the fine and yellow silky streams coming out of the bakery's ovens; the rough and black woollen streams coming out of the cremation ovens.

When emerging freely into the cold air, those traces of nutrition and death merge into a single billow that joins the permanent clouds, adding to the grey.

The union of industry and meteorology. The joining of water vapour and the smoke of profit.

The Worker is on the cusp of crying. But not there, not in public. He holds back his tears. The Worker knows that to cry in the middle of the road is to be nude. To expose one's insides to greedy eyes. Crying is fine, but alone, in a room with the door locked from the inside.

Because there are people who not only feed on dead meat. They also slake their thirst in the pools made by the eyes of the living.

Different wings – the jewel of our cuisine

In the Factory's south wing, animals are slaughtered. Skinned and cleaned, then minced. The pastry dough is made with flour, yeast, butter and salt. After being allowed to rise, the leavened dough is wrapped around the minced meat, which has been braised with onions. After a final lacquering with egg, the baking trays are greased and then . . . into the oven.

The meat pies grow inside the ovens to quieten people's stomachs. And to act as a form of currency. Whenever they eat these meat pies, members of the Government sing the praises of this *jewel of our cuisine* that is also an engine of economic growth.

In the Factory's north wing, death burns. The vestiges of those who can no longer eat are extinguished. The former eaters and digesters enter that wing as corpses, like the animals in the south wing after they have been put down. After being undressed, washed and weighed, the corpses are put into the cremation ovens to be reduced to the humility of dust.

No braising, no lacquering with egg, no greasing of baking trays.

The main difference between the two wings, beyond their economic value, the ingredients and utensils they employ, or the smells they release, is in the power of their ovens. In the temperature required for each of the activities: baking and incinerating. And in the time needed to arrive at the final product.

For the meat pies, the ovens are heated to approximately 200 degrees Celsius, and it takes 40 minutes for the pastry to be crispy.

In the cremation process, the thermometer rises to almost four digits. 950 degrees Celsius.

And it takes 120 minutes to reduce a 90-kilogramme corpse to 400 grammes of ashes.

This is what some call baking to death.

The power to grope

From the security cabin, officers watch the proletariat entering the Factory. The Worker mingles with the throng. Men, women, children, expatriates, foreigners, refugees of war exchange glances like tame cattle.

With tenderness and with resentment, the Worker watches couples as they let go of each other's hands and kiss goodbye.

At the Factory's entrance, the two groups that from time immemorial have insisted on preserving our strange species must separate: men through the left door, women through the right. They are not allowed to work together. Only when the shift is over will they be reunited to re-establish the natural order of things.

Men and women embrace pointlessly.

The Worker clears his throat.

Love . . .

The rest of the sentence remains unsaid.

Hidden out of sight by a modesty barrier, men, women and children are screened. Patted down by hands that can be rough or gentle, depending on the carnal inclination of whoever is doing the handling. There had been complaints, from the men, women and children, sent to the Head of the Security Department, against some guards accused of showing excessive zeal, of taking advantage of the power to grope. But all those grievance notes had been read and crumpled and promptly shoved into a plastic bag and thrown into the fire.

Often followed by the threat of reprisals, the complaints soon diminished until they, too, were reduced to ashes and complicit silence.

To see your crow caw

From adolescence, persistent acne had covered his face like pimpled wallpaper. Because a man's face is his calling card, the Worker always supposed that his repellent appearance would prevent anyone from feeling attracted to him. How wrong he was. Luckily for him, ugliness can be as alluring as beauty. And that Guard with the porky figure had now fallen into the net.

The Guard is plump. Thin neck. Skin red and mottled like a sausage. Every day, when he sees the Worker approaching, his hands tremble with anticipation and his lips curl into a malicious smile. With a hooked finger, the Guard says, *come closer.* He licks his moustache. He winks before feeling up the Worker with motherly tenderness: confirming that the muscles are toned, and the bones are intact. But, mostly, confirming the hardness of the buttocks and the bulk of the genitals.

When the display of tenderness is over, and as the Worker cynically prepares to go through the motions of opening up his bag for inspection – as you can see, I have nothing to hide – the Guard waves him through with a fluttering hand and watering eyes.

It has been like that since the Messenger ordered the Worker to remain open to the Guard's advances.

But things had moved on. Once, while his fellow guards were busy, their own hungry hands probing other people's bodies, the Guard had surprised him. He had put a parcel in his hands.

Hours later, after his shift, the Worker had cut the string and unwrapped the parcel to find two pies, an apple and a note that said:

I want to see your crow caw again.

The Worker could not stop smiling as he read those words. The poetic reference to the tattoo on his left buttock was a sign. Once again, the Messenger's instinct had been correct: beyond sating the beast's appetite, the exchange of fluids and grunts with the puffy Guard would be very useful to their cause when summer came.

And then the Worker scoffed the pies and the apple.

In the City, hunger does not show its teeth. But then again, how can one measure hunger? What scale can be used to measure want? The kilos of hankering or the grammes of malnutrition? Even in earlier times there was no abundance: since the Great Disaster, meat had been a Government monopoly; fish was scarce, the sea was distant. But there had been vegetables and pulses for soup, and grains for bread. Food, though rationed, found its way into all stomachs.

Only the residents of the Blue Zone – top military brass and, above, all members of Government – had access to fresh fruit, fine cuts of beef, yoghurt and, of course, the meat pies.

Things we do for a new eye

Tenth day after the Messenger's arrest.

Beyond the Wall, in the Hospital, the Blond Doctor holds up a hand mirror. And in his other hand, using two fingers, tweezers.

Cross-legged on the green velvet chair, he plucks and weeds.

The Blond Doctor refers to the unruly hairs determined to grow on the wrong parts of his face as weeds.

Sitting in the patient's chair, the executioner with the glass eye watches with embarrassment. He coughs. Pulls out a hand-kerchief. Spits into it. Examines it.

Plucking yet another hair off the perfect curve, the Blond Doctor says:

God doesn't know how to design eyebrows.

Eyebrows or anything else.

What do you mean?

He's a bad architect. He didn't know how to make people.

Is that what you think?

Yes! Just think about this, Doctor: how many times did *He* and *His* holy dove need to come down to Earth, up and down, up and down – even the dove must have been dizzy – only to hand out some form of punishment, until *He* got tired and real-ised it wasn't worth it? How many times? Do you, Doctor, think that if *He*'d known how to make people properly, *He* would have had all that work? All that sending of plagues and fires? *He* even had to nail his son to a cross. Like I said, not good at eyebrows or anything else. *He*'s a bad architect.

Yes . . . You may be right . . . I think they're done. What do you think?

I really can't say, Doctor.

You should pluck too.

Me?

Yes. Your eyebrows. So, you'll have two, instead of that single fat one. You'll look prettier.

Prettier?

And if I were you, I'd take the opportunity to pluck those black weeds sprouting from your ears and nostrils.

Black weeds?

Yes. The hairs. What's wrong with that?

Well . . . I don't know . . .

Fine . . . Enough about the pesky weeds . . . I called you because I wanted to say, personally, that I'm very pleased with you.

Sir?

I'm very pleased with you.

Thank you.

You did a good job in the Forest. You'll be rewarded. You deserve it.

Well . . . Uh . . . I was just doing my job . . . It was nothing . . . Yes . . . I mean . . . I was only doing what you asked me to . . . And now you'll get me a new eye?

Patience . . . Let's be patient, shall we? And do things properly.

But you promised, Doctor.

I promised and I'll keep the promise. You know I'm a man of my word.

I know.

I'm a man of my word.

Yes, Doctor.

I am, am I not?

Yes.

The thing is . . . the thing is this: I haven't yet found a compatible donor.

You haven't?

But I'll find one. Don't you worry. You know I'm a man of my word. It's just a matter of time. We have to be patient.

I'm patient.

Good. I can guarantee that, when you least expect it, it will happen. And you'll have a new eye. But I still need you to do another job for me.

A new coughing fit makes Glass Eye bend over. He stands up to regain his breath. When he sits down again, he swallows hard to stave off another coughing fit.

The Blond Doctor has taken advantage of the coughing to put his tweezers and mirror into the drawer. He licks a fingertip and traces his freshly plucked eyebrow.

I'm sorry, Doctor . . . This cough isn't getting any better.

You've taken your tablets?

Yes.

How often?

Every eight hours.

I'll give you an expectorant bronchodilator to help you clear the phlegm.

A broncho . . . what?

A cough syrup.

Is it bitter? If it's bitter, I can't get it down.

Don't worry, it's sweet.

That's good . . . But . . . Please continue, Doctor, my cough interrupted you.

You drew up a map, didn't you?

I did.

After that thing.

I did. After that thing. Like you ordered, Doctor.

And you marked on the map the place where you buried him?

Yes, with a red X.

Excellent. So now you'll take that map and hand it to the Messenger.

That bastard . . . But . . .

Now you'll take that map and hand it to the Messenger. You'll do exactly as I say.

Yes, but . . . How will I . . . ? I'm sorry, Doctor, but to do that . . . With that giant there . . . Not sure if you understand . . . What you're asking me to do . . .

Tell me: do you want a new eye, or don't you?

I do.

Do you really want it?

Yes.

Why?

Well . . . I'm fed up with my wife calling me a *one-eyed bastard*. And with my children looking at my glass eye with fear.

So there!

Yes.

Get the map you made into those warty hands. Without the giant knowing about it.

Well . . . That'll be the difficult part.

No, it won't. Don't you worry. Words are powerful. They can open and close doors. All will be well, you'll see.

You're sure?

I'm certain. Didn't you do that thing in the Forest?

I did.

And you did it well, didn't you?

If you say so, Doctor . . .

Give him the map you made. The Messenger will know what to do. And you'll be rewarded.

Rewarded?

Yes.

With a new eye, Doctor?

A lovely eye. Trust me. You have my word.

Behold, I am sending you out like wolves among lambs

In the Factory's changing rooms, the door to cubicle 161 opens. The Worker, like other workers, takes off his personal clothes to put on a white butcher's smock. (Why white, when the main matter is blood?) After hanging his clothes on a hanger, and putting away the suitcase, the Worker gazed into the mirror. Using the fingers of his left hand, he combed back his blond fringe. And he was no longer the same man.

In that gesture of acceptance, in the simple act of taking off one personal garment to put on another, a uniform, was a transformation not only of the exterior but also of the mind. The Worker had to stop thinking and acting like an ordinary man to start thinking and acting like a butcher. Brother among brothers. Who, dressed in white butchers' smocks, comprised the brotherhood of butchers.

In his immaculate smock, he roamed the corridor towards the building in which the slaughterhouse was located.

Foot traffic was frantic as shifts changed. A methodical hubbub rose from the hundreds of rubber soles of the workers, wearing away the linoleum as they walked. Unintelligible words, in a constant murmur, passed from mouth to mouth. An alignment of yellow lights, attached to the roof, simulated full moons, beneath which the wolves in lambs' clothes exchanged their tales.

Sullied smocks were replaced by clean ones.

And so it was: some left, splattered in blood, while others arrived, clean and innocent for the time being.

Behold, I am sending you out like wolves among lambs.

At the end of the corridor, the Worker pulled the facemask's elastic loops around his ears. The facemask was a fine barrier against the stench of corruption. Finally, and before taking up his post in the carousel of killing, he took one final glimpse at the sharpened and shimmering blade of his butcher's knife. From where he was, he could already hear the lowing of animals, anticipating something imminent and, for one last time, making the most of being alive.

The gentle treadmill

They are not asked for their opinions. The animals exit their metal holding pens in single file like obedient students. They sniff each other's tails. Sniffing tails is one way to find their bearings.

Using rods, the workers direct them towards the treadmill. The treadmill moves slowly so the animals won't trip. Once they have stepped onto the rolling path, with obedient legs, they cannot turn back. They cannot avoid the destination that the gentle treadmill guides them towards.

The destination is a large box.

During their journey, despite the comfort, the animals low. They growl. Demonic songs.

The large box has two doors.

At the entrance, a curtain of plastic strips welcomes them, licking their hides. At the exit, another similar curtain wishes them farewell, licking the fallen bodies. The plastic strip curtains hang equidistant over the two doors. Their purpose: to hide what happens inside the box. The only thing that is known is that the animals are still singing when they enter, but they are peacefully mute as they exit.

A small click separates those two moments.

Singing and muteness.

A click like a switch being turned on and off.

Entering the box.
Click.
Exiting the box.
The click makes all the difference.

The Bald Minister bites a pie

11:19.
Blue Zone.
Government Tower.
7th Floor.

Inside the Bald Minister's office, the temperature is around 22 degrees Celsius. There is the constant murmur of the air conditioner.

The Bald Minister is at ease. Because of the agreeable temperature and also because, only two weeks after ordering the Messenger's arrest, neither the sound of wagging tongues nor of adrenaline-fuelled hearts can be heard in the City. The people no longer speak of wolves, or of the Devil, or of premonitions. With this silence, and the physical absence of the metaphysical agitator, life within the Walls is re-established. And back to its organised harshness.

The Bald Minister opens a drawer. He pulls out a box of blue tablets. Pops two of them into his mouth. Drinks water.

The Secretary with brown eyes lined with black eyeliner comes into the office with a tray filled with steaming hot pies.

After biting into one of the crusty pies, the Bald Minister says to the Secretary:

Dance.

Now?

Yes. Seeing you dance helps me digest better. And helps me come up with new laws.

The pie's juices run down the Bald Minister's jaw and onto the silk pyjama's top.

The Secretary hesitates. In the past, the Bald Minister had turned on the radio. She says:

It's difficult like that, Minister, without the music . . . May I turn the radio on?

The Bald Minister stops chewing. Meat sticks to his teeth. His reptile tongue explores the gaps between them. And grinding his jaws, in a fatty voice, he replies:

I asked you to dance. Not to turn the radio on. There's enough music in your body. You just need to listen harder. So, I'll tell you again: dance, dance, dance, dance . . .

The executioners talk (II): There were five the day before yesterday

In the Persuasion Suite, Glass Eye, sitting on the purple velvet chair, is having coughing fits. He puts the handkerchief to his mouth. Examines it.

After clearing his lungs, he lights a cigarette. Takes two drags.

He says to Neck Brace, who, sitting on an uncomfortable chair, is gazing into the fish tank, mesmerised:

Want one?
Not now.
This cough is killing me.
Sounds bad.
It is. Just look at this shit.
You have to see a doctor.
I have.
And?
He gave me some yellow pills and some syrup.
Sweet?
Strawberry flavoured.
Lucky you.
I know. I told him that if it was bitter, I couldn't swallow it.
It'll kick in soon.
That's what he said. But it's been *kicking in soon* for a week.
It's a well-known fact.

What is?

That it takes a while . . . It takes a while to work. It won't happen overnight.

Yes, but it's been over a week.

I know. Don't worry. It'll happen soon.

Did you know the guy plucks his eyebrows?

The Blond Doctor?

And he gets manicures.

I don't trust that guy.

Yes . . . Neither do I . . . Neither do I . . . Believe me . . . Want a pie? I have half a dozen. The Small Man got them for me.

I do, but I'm not sure my stomach will thank me.

Glass Eye lets out a long billow of smoke.

He looks at Neck Brace. Clears his throat.

And you . . . Your neck any better?

It's been worse.

Right. So, you're improving.

That's not what I said.

What did you say?

I said: it's been worse.

How so?

It's worse at night. In the daytime I can cope. But at night, I just can't find the right position in bed. Nothing works. I'm in pain when I turn one way, I'm in pain when I turn another. It's intolerable. I have to take a handful of tablets to take the pain away.

What colour?

The green ones.

That's a pity. It's a crying shame, that's what it is.

It is.

It's not good when you start taking too many of them.

Exactly . . . That's it . . . That's it! . . . I knew it! . . . I knew it! . . . There's only four left! The day before yesterday there were five! That's what's different!

What are you talking about?
The fish tank . . . Look . . .

The phone rings.

Glass Eye stubs out his cigarette on the sole of his boot, puts the cigarette butt into his shirt pocket, answers the phone:

Hello.

. . .

Yes.

. . .

In fifteen minutes.

. . .

Fine.

. . .

Not bringing him up here.

. . .

Yes, understood.

He hangs up.

In the executioner's face, the glass eye, dead, is shining more brightly than ever.

It was the giant.

So, do we need to get started?

No, we won't be persuading the Messenger.

No?

No.

How so?

Don't know.

Why?

Don't know. The giant wouldn't say. Can you believe this shit?

And only yesterday we spent two hours arguing until we agreed that the 'Tiger's bench' would be the next tool of persuasion . . .

Can you believe it? This is a stitch-up. That's what this is. A bloody stitch-up. I just don't get it. Really. The world's gone mad.

The warty man got to him.

You think?

He got to him. The man got to him. Can't you see it?

Yes. Yes. That's it. You're right . . . That's it . . . You're right. The bastard got to him.

Or perhaps he hasn't been able to speak because of his teeth . . .

Yes . . . The teeth . . . Or . . . The giant chickened out because of all the talk about the Redhead.

The Redhead, yes. For sure.

You heard what the bastard said, didn't you?

The two executioners exchange complicit glances.

That the Giant does not have the fingers to satisfy the Redhead.

They let out loud laughs.

Neck Brace composes himself.

I'd forgotten about that . . .

Right, my boy. We should know better. No laughing allowed here.

No laughing?

No laughing.

And how do we do that?

What?

Not laughing. When I can't help it . . .

Who knows. Look . . . Try crying. It won't hurt as much.

Stop making fun of me.

Sure.

But seriously, isn't it strange . . . ?

Who knows . . . Only the giant knows . . . He must have his reasons.

No, not that . . . I'm sure. Yesterday there were five in the fish tank.

Five?

Five fish. I'm certain. I counted them. And today there are only four. There's an orange one missing.

What orange one?

The orange fish with the crooked fin.

The dead come in, the pies come out

It is happening there, now.

It happened yesterday. It will happen tomorrow.

It happens because it needs to happen.

Every day the gates of the Factory's south wing open to let death in. Death is the definitive answer.

The dead enter the same way the pies leave: in two batches – at dawn and at dusk. Grey wagons with the Government's star printed onto the greyness are in charge of pickups, transportation and delivery.

High up in one of the offices of the Government Tower, adapted specifically for that purpose, phones ring. Whoever picks up takes note of the suspected death. After going through the motions of expressing condolences comes a detailed questionnaire, for any future inquest, and then a time is agreed for a pickup.

Before the agreed time – any delay is punishable – four armed men in grey uniforms arrive, wearing facemasks and gloves. They ring doorbells. They knock on doors. Then, a cousin, an aunt, a brother, a grandmother, a nephew, a widow, a mother-in-law, a widower, a brother-in-law, a son, will turn the door handle, the key, the latch, and the four men will enter.

They know immediately where to go: follow the crying. One of the men, the head of operations, will make his way towards the room with the mourners and expel them with shouts and thuggish gestures. After the orders, the tearful relatives huddle beneath the door frame. Though their eyesight is still blurred with emotion, they do not want to miss the last moments of those who lie so still.

The head of operations approaches the body. He pulls back the blanket. Notes the body's position. Opens the deceased's eyelids like someone might open windows. Using a small torch, he peers into the pupils. After observing the dilation, he shuts the windows. He then takes out of his bag a syringe with no needle. He injects cold water into one of the ears. Waits fifteen seconds. Grabs the blue ears, and shakes the immobile head: left, right. He sticks a long needle in the tight space between a finger and a fingernail, or between a toe and a toenail. Every one of these operations has the ability to suspend, briefly, the floods of tears from the perturbed eyes following the perform-ance closely from beneath the door frame. They also bring to those upset hearts a new hope. As if something extraordinary were about to happen. A pointless hope, that the person they had loved or hated so much might make an unexpected gesture and get up suddenly.

Finally, using a stethoscope, the head of operations listens for a heartbeat. The last examination. Silence touches the walls. After hearing the hollowness, he says in a sharp voice:

Death confirmed.

Two men approach and wrap the body in a blanket. The cries and lamentations of relatives huddled beneath the door frame begin again, abruptly, as if the engine of grief had been stuck in neutral and waiting for a signal to continue its way. Besides the bed or somewhere on the living room floor, the fourth man stretches out and unzips a canvas bag, into which the corpse – now confirmed as such – is placed and sealed.

A yellow sticker with a number and time of collection is stuck onto the canvas bag. The head of operations hands a blue form to one of the relatives.

When the form has been signed, the original kept for the files, the duplicate left with the relatives, the four men leave just as they arrived. Precise, hurried, professional. Now carrying a heavy bundle.

For the men in grey uniforms, dealing with death is like moving furniture. *The thing* needs to be moved from one place to another. Nothing more.

The vans arrive at the Factory.

They back up into the drop-off hangar. The back doors open wide, and the canvas-wrapped bundles are thrown onto empty stretchers. Workers from the South Zone, marker in hand, check the stickers. They write down the number on a green sheet of paper that is then signed by the person in charge of collection, transport and delivery.

The van doors are shut. Engines are ignited. The smoke spewed out of exhaust pipes heralds the future of those who, zipped up in canvas bags, inert and mute, are no longer asking any questions.

Because they have had a definitive answer.

That is how it is:

It happened there, a short while ago.

It also happened yesterday. And it will happen tomorrow.

It happened because it needs to happen.

The shaking of a gloveless hand (I):
How to make a puddle that size?

The Director had time for a fertile hate-filled thought before entering the Prison cell. Walking down the narrow corridor, flanked by the guard, he recalled the shape of the puddle of urine on the linoleum floor. How was that even possible? An insignificant wretch like that able to produce a puddle of piss that size? Did he himself have to be subjected to torture to be able to piss properly once again? And the prisoner's ironic tone when he talked about *the Redhead*? About how she would *give it up* and *enjoy it*? Or about *prosthetics*? Unacceptable!

While the guard unlocked the door, the Director mulled over giving him another chance, the last one, to explain himself, before signing the sentence.

The Director had to admit: after the Messenger's unsuccessful interview, and the subsequent persuasion, heavy doubts had been hammering away at him. His head and his heart, each employing its own method, took turns tormenting him. The Director's head was an alarm clock about to go off. His heart, overloaded and unrelenting, played like a piano. His head: tick-tock, tick-tock. And his heart: plink-plink, plink-plink. Tick-tock up high. Plink-plink further below. Added to the drip-drip of disability . . . Let us agree . . . It was not easy to start his days. Or to get through his nights.

Ultimately:

How did the Messenger know about the Director's *loss*?

And what did he mean by him *recovering them*?

And the Redhead? Who had, or would, she be spreading her legs for?

Back then, the Director had observed the prisoner's gestures with precision; and his hands had not lied. They had been sincere. Not even the smallest of hesitations. And now, there he was again, standing in front of the prisoner, feeling naked, his secrets exposed, gloves behind his back, faced with the mystery, the evil, the fear, not knowing how to address it.

I wash exshpecting you, Director.

The Messenger spoke in a new accent, having lost his two front teeth, lying on a cot, hands behind his head, eyes filled with provocation.

I knew you were coming. What'sh wrong? Do come in. Will you shtand there in shilenshe? You can come in and ashk queshtions. Today I'll anshwer. Not the shame queshtions from the other day. Othersh. Different queshtions. You know the onesh. Sho? What do you want to know firsht, Director?

The Director took two steps. He entered the cell. He tried to control his breathing and his jangling nerves. The Messenger sat up on the cot. He cracked his knuckles. Patted the thin mattress: a polite invitation. His face still bore the marks of the persuasion: bruises and dry blood.

Come, don't jusht shtay there! Let'sh make a deal. You ashk me a question. Jusht one. And I'll give you the right anshwer. Then you give me shomething in return. That'sh the deal. I will tell you one of the many thingsh you want to know. Then, if all goesh well, you can ashk another queshtion. What do you want to know firsht, Director? Where your fingersh are? Or who the Redhead is sheeing? Shall we make a deal?

And he put out a warty hand.
  The Director watched him closely, standing over him.
  Despite the warts, it was an honest hand.

The shaking of a gloveless hand (II): Let'sh make a deal?

Observing the extended hand, held aloft, as if poised on an invisible tabletop, offering itself, the Director felt sharp misgivings. And he felt ashamed of all his thoughts. Disgust, loathing, of himself, of what was in his head. One can never truly know a man. Evil has many disguises. He turned suddenly and, using only his eyes and eyebrows, lied to the guard posted outside the cell door, saying: you can go, I've got everything under control.

The Director raised his gloves to his face as he admired the hand, thin, immobile, gaunt, with no protruding veins. He combed his beard with one of the false fingers. He felt the pressure of the hard prosthetic finger. But the finger's hardness did not feel the face's softness. Never in all his years had he found himself inside a cell in a position of disadvantage. The Director was now pondering the real likelihood of emerging defeated from this combat, instead of a victor. The Messenger, tired of hesitation, straightened his shoulders and showed his new gappy smile:

Not shure what to ashk firsht, right? I undershtand. It'sh a difficult choishe: the fingersh, or the Redhead? All choishes are difficult. I know that very well. I alsho had to make a choishe. And it washn't eashy, trusht me. The trick is to acshept what we are given. Think, Director . . . Follow my reashoning: with no fingersh, you lose the Redhead, right? But if you get them back, who knowsh? I know what will happen nexsht . . . It'sh up to you . . . If you want to know firsht who the Redhead ish shee-ing . . . But that will only delay recovering the digitsh that you need so badly. Beshides, I've already drawn the map . . .

What map?

The Director's lower jaw dropped with the weight of his amazement. The Messenger lifted the mattress and pulled out a folded sheet of paper. He unfolded it like a magician performing a trick that requires deliberate slowness, and he smiled again.

Thish map! You can shee here, Director! Thish ish where they are! Your belongingsh! Your treasure! But that is only half the map. The other half I'll give you when you have fulfilled my demandsh.

You're mad!

Me?

You're lying!

No need to get overexshited. Watch out for your heart . . .

What I'll do is sign the order, so that you're up against that grey wall and in front of the firing squad!

You won't do that, Director.

We'll see!

Calm down. Don't get overexshited. You won't do that, Director. Let'sh make a deal: take thish half of the map. But I ashk for four things in return. Firsht: put me in a new shell, thish one ish too shmall. And the matresh, goodnesh! Try shleeping here a single night and you'll shee what shtate your sphine ish in when you wake up. Shecond: find me a dentisht. To replace the teeth you keep in your pocket. You keep them there, don't you? You play with them when you're alone ash if they were coinsh? But you know, Director, thoshe thingsh in your pocket aren't coinsh.

*

The Director put his hand in his right pocket. He felt three drops dripping from his urethra. A strong stinging sensation in his perineum. The Messenger continued.

Third: I want you to authorishe a vishit from a Worker at the Factory. I'll write down hish name. Fourth and final: get me a copy of the holy book. If there ish anywhere that God ish needed, surely it ish here. That'sh it. That'sh my lisht. It'sh a fair deal. You give me thoshe four thingsh. I give you the misshing part of the map sho you can dig out your four fingersh. Better to dig them out before the shummer, that'sh if you want to recover them in time . . . Ash you can shee, Director, I'm not ashking for anything that ishn't within your powersh. I'm not even ashking to be released. For now, only those four thingsh. You'll shee how everything goesh well.

You're mad! Completely mad!

The Messenger came close to the Director. He raised his chin. He hid the hand with the half map behind his back and pointed the other hand at the Director's navel. A weapon ready to be jabbed into the abdomen.

You know very well that I'm not. I wash jusht choshen.

Chosen?

Yesh. *He* choshe me and I couldn't do anything about that. You're clever. That'sh why I advishe you: pull off the glovesh. And shake my hand like a man. Let'sh make a deal. Hand in hand. And I'll give you this half of the map.

The Director looked into the Messenger's eyes and could not see a trace of fear, or anger. Only an irritating serenity. And his hand, though ugly, was truly sincere.

The dawn of a new law

Snow strikes the morning with its open hand.

Windows shout: winter.

And inside his office in the Government Tower, the Bald Minister, sitting on the leather sofa in silk pyjamas, having studied the Factory's productivity rates and the Brown Zone's criminality records, uncrossed his legs.

Indifferent to the temperature outside, the Bald Minister yawns before reaching a decision as he sits below the air conditioner vent: lukewarm air blows over his baldness and his ideas.

The decision is about a new law that aims to reduce evil and laziness in the hearts of those who live in the Brown Zone and work in the Factory.

The Bald Minister believes there may be an incestuous relationship between laziness and evil. Between the mattress springs and the knife of delinquency.

After taking out the cotton balls from between his toes, and feeling the false breeze on his smooth pate, the Bald Minister feels ready to start dictation. The Bald Minister prefers to dictate laws and other thoughts instead of writing them by hand.

He says:

The hand is not speedy enough to keep up with the pace of a thinking man; it is not speedy enough to capture the mist of imagination. And thoughts become stale, imagination vanishes into thin air, if the hand is not speedy enough.

*

The Bald Minister, with his peculiar subterranean voice, began voicing his thoughts out loud. Sitting in front of him, his Assistant wrote them down in a notepad, as quickly as the Minister dictated, at the speed he had learned to attain on the roads of the Bald Minister's ideas.

The dictation: The place where love and evil fornicate

In the Brown Zone there are still people who have time in their hearts. People with too many hours to spend on leisure and laziness. And this encourages evil, as well as slowing down economic progress. If only those people had ticking clocks inside their bodies instead of toothsome hearts.

After writing down this phrase, the Assistant could not help smiling at the Bald Minister. Who continued delicately rolling the cotton balls he kept pulling out from between his toes, before sniffing them as if they were flowers.

Yes, clocks instead of hearts: precise mechanisms made from metal cogs instead of arteries and veins. If that were the case, everything would be easier. But no. There are men who insist on winding up their hearts. The hearts of men are machines in need of tuning, cannibalistic. Machines to eat other men.

When a given person, on a given day, engages with another; when that given person makes a new friend, or a lover, and celebrates and drinks and laughs with that other person on that given day, he cannot possibly wish to destroy the other person at dawn of the following day. And yet that is what happens. And the more time that person has to give in to idleness, to inertia, to the feeling of volatility, the worse it is.

The world's great philosophies were born of idleness but

stimulate apathy. And we all know about the human wretchedness caused by the disastrous implementation of those great philosophies in daily human life. And then there is that most dangerous of times – considered a priority by many – that people like to spend on 'family'. Despite us knowing statistically – and the numbers are there for whoever needs to see them – that 'family' is that place we choose, with anxious walls and complaining bedsprings, for love and for evil to share a bed.

Where love and evil fornicate.

I ask: is it true that people are more productive when they are happier?

Is happiness productive?

And the family? Is it one of the essential nerves helping the economic muscle to contract and expand and grow?

Who are you trying to kid?

Family, and leisure, are a farce. The masks for delinquency. There is more hatred and resentment in the whites of certain family members' eyes than there is among enemy soldiers who find themselves face to face in the trenches. That is because they have had enough time to annoy and bore each other; to contaminate each other with vulgarity; a vulgarity that sticks to the bones like caramel; a caramel that blocks arteries and dislodges the mechanisms of productivity. All of this because some people had extra hours to practise the evil of love and the love of evil. Thus, I consider it a matter of urgency to revoke Article 175 of our legislation, which enshrines the right to weekly rest. And applying equal zeal to the one employed in the revocation, I order the swift implementation of a new law that will suppress definitively the single day of weekly rest for all Factory workers and residents of the Brown Zone. This way, productivity will increase, and criminality will diminish.

Thus did the Bald Minister dictate.

Thus did the Assistant write it all down in his notebook.

With the final full stop in place, the Bald Minister scratched the inside of his ear with his little finger. He picked up the phone and ordered that the law be implemented, effective immediately. He tore a random page out of the Book of Laws and cleaned off the earwax he had just scraped out with his fingernail, and then threw the scrunched-up piece of paper into a waste basket.

The Assistant left the Bald Minister's office with a sense of duty fulfilled: a firm and impeccable smile, and a newly promulgated law under his arm.

Eight metres of greyness

Wherever they look – north, south, east, west – any pair of eyes will come across those eight metres of greyness. The Wall imposes itself. It obliterates any horizon. There is whatever stands between us and the eight metres of greyness. And then there is what is beyond our vision, in the distance.

The concrete barrier is interrupted only by four steel gates, strategically placed. Where the garrisoned guards, dressed in blue uniforms, carrying grey weapons, watch over the traffic of goods and people.

Because of his profession, and because he lives in the Blue Zone, it is easy to think of the Director as privileged. In one of his pockets, he carries – like all who live beneath blue roofs – a pass that allows him to enter any Zone or cross any border in the City without having to answer any questions. He can go in and out of the Wall, whenever and as often as he wants.

But this apparent freedom leaves the Director indifferent. It puts neither a smile on his lips nor sadness in his eyes. As far as his own freedom of movement is concerned, being able to choose a street, or a Zone, the Director considers himself to be somewhere between a slave and a tyrant. That is because he knows that when he passes beyond this Wall, he will find, further on, another one, perhaps higher. And, having passed that other one, there will be yet one more, perhaps thicker. Even when one Wall comes down on the left side of the world, on the

right side there will soon be foundations, formwork and concrete poured in large quantities to raise a new hard curtain.

A world without walls, without curtains, is not believable.
  Because there is no world without fears.
  Walls, curtains, are the architecture of fear.
  And the fear is us.
  Thus spoke the Director.

Learning to see – when Hell touches us with an unexpected wing

The Great Disaster eliminated over two thirds of the population. It destroyed buildings, laws and minds considered solid up to that point. It forced the survivors – the beneficiaries of randomness – to make do with what remains of destruction: dust.

The Director was nine years old and still full of dreams when his father took his hand, minutes after the *accident*, and led him for a walk around the ruins as if they were visiting a garden filled with rare plants and trees. With the shouts and the exhalations of smoke still fresh amid the devastation, his father forced him not to shut off his senses. So that the son would register with the eye of memory the shadows of human fragility and, at the same time, of human arrogance.

Squeezing his hand tightly, the father said:

Don't turn your eyes away. Look and learn. So that you never forget.

It has to be said: only when Hell touches us with an unexpected wing do we open our eyes.

In fact, that was the first mental photograph taken by the Director as a child. Because whenever he went back in time, whenever he rooted around in the disorganised library of the past, his memories stopped there. In that still and pure image of devastation.

It was on the day of the Great Disaster, and guided by his father's strong hand, that the Director opened his eyes fully for the first time.

At the age of nine, the Director learned to see.

The frenemy

The Wall was built after the Great Disaster. And his father was the engineer in charge. An inherited awareness of that project still runs through the Director's bloodstream.

All of us, without exception, whenever expressing admiration or rage about that hard concrete curtain that prevents *some* residents from carrying out *some* movements, are also praising or insulting the mind and the hands of the man that built it.

As the one and only legitimate son, the Director still feels the reverberations of his father's authority.

But beyond the pride in his heritage, the Director does not give the Wall the importance that others do: the Wall is part of the landscape. And the Director has become as used to its shadow as to the daily lentil soup, or the Son tethered to the piano, or the Redhead's tightly shuttered legs, or even, at a stretch, the loss of his fingers.

The Director thinks of the Wall as a necessary evil, inevitable. He thinks:

The problem is not that evil does not come alone.

The problem is: it comes often, and always accompanied. And when it does, the company it keeps is even more seductive than evil itself, which does not like to walk alone.

That is why, instead of the eight metres of greyness, or any other external barrier, the Director's energy and attention are focused on the most insurmountable – though fragile – of all barriers, the *frenemy* we carry with us at all times: our mortal body.

That is right: the mortal body. Consider, for instance, the Director's recent urinary issues.

What relevance can an eight-metre wall have alongside a permanent inability to piss?

The mutilated writing

No one so far – except for the fish, dying of boredom in the fish tank – has had the privilege of watching him skilfully and secretly execute his handwriting.

It was strange, and also thrilling, to witness the way in which, using only his three fingers pressed against each other, the Director held the pen to produce perfect calligraphy. Slightly sloping. Curves linking one verb to another. Deftly and patiently joining the lines that make up consonants and vowels.

It is doubtful that even the greatest graphological scholar would be able to distinguish in the freedom of that handwriting the signs of mutilation: both of the hand, and of its owner's character. In any case, the Director wrote easily, quickly, without hesitation: forging an experienced heart.

Making sure the door was shut, he undressed his left hand. The suede glove, inanimate, placed next to the living hand. Just then, the fish in the fish tank stopped moving: they kissed the tank's glass and with hypnotic eyes followed the side-to-side movement of the defective hand scratching the paper in search of the best words. Life or death. Death or life. The fruit or the stone. Stone or fruit. Always the same melody (hidden like a mimetic insect) on the white paper of existence.

Though disabled, that hand was still powerful.

It sometimes happened that, as he wrote, the Director would be overcome by an irrepressible urge to cry, without knowing the reason why.

His amoral hand wrote speedily, with determination, and the Director cried tears. How many times did he turn his head away so that they would not smudge the ink? So that the emotion-filled drops of liquid did not stain the rational decision.

Even having suffered mutilation, when he wrote, and only when he wrote, did the Director feel, for a moment, that his body was complete, free, faultless.

Will you be asking me any more questions, Director? (Case file 1716)

Sitting in the purple velvet chair in the Persuasion Suite, the Director was finalising files and putting his signature to sentences. The Director was the penultimate piece in the game of condemning someone to an execution. The piece that falls, or fails to, bringing things to their conclusion. This case file, number 1716, reached an easy conclusion: death by firing squad. These were the words scribbled on the case file's bottom corner. It had never been as easy for the Director to write death by firing squad.

The woman in question, a resident of the Grey Zone, with bird-like nose and chipped fingernails, had stabbed her husband twenty-one times. Twenty-one. And then, with hands and clothes soaked in blood, she had drowned her two young daughters in the bath.

The Director has asked the homicidal woman three questions. Her persuasive replies, alongside her gesticulation, were recorded in the case file as follows:

1. Why? He used to beat me with a shoe. We no longer talked. He never asked me anything. Unlike you, Director, asking questions now. He didn't. Does that seem normal? Not wanting to hear what I had to say? And that's not all: he wouldn't buy me cigarettes. And he beat me with a shoe whenever I asked him

for a cigarette. He didn't love me. Only he could smoke, the bastard! And besides, his breathing was horrendous. I couldn't get a moment's respite: he snored like a sick animal.

2. My girls ... I don't know ... I don't know ... I don't know ... I couldn't take any more. I couldn't sleep. For months, I hadn't had a full night's sleep, uninterrupted. If one started crying, the other would kick off in imitation. And I would get up. I was doing it on my own. Because the bastard was just snoring. And my girls wouldn't stop crying or shitting outside of the potty. My girls ... They made me nervous. I don't know ... I think I just wanted them to stop crying and shitting outside of the potty.

3. I tried to find the revolver. I turned the house upside down and couldn't find it. He had hidden it on purpose. I still don't know where. That son of a bitch didn't trust me. He didn't love me. He wanted me to spread my legs without ever asking. He beat me with a shoe. Director: he never asked me any questions. Does that seem normal? Will you be asking me any more questions, Director?

How to look after a fish (I)

He used a small net to scoop it out of the Prison fish tank and smuggled it out, floating in a plastic bag, inside his anorak pocket.

Once home, he asked the short-sighted Maid for a porcelain tureen.

The following morning the fish came up to the surface. It opened and closed its mouth, asking for food. Its fins danced around hopefully. Hunger, though it be a friend of death, is also a melody that belongs in life.

Pressing the remains of a ginger muffin between two fingers, the Director sprinkled crumbs into the tureen. And, using his middle finger, he crushed a pink tablet against the lid. Once it was crushed, he sprinkled the powder into the water.

The Director was feeding the fish only to poison it immediately.

That was the game: these crumbs, or those?

The muffin or the tablet?

Food or an anxiolytic?

The fish made a choice. It had free will. Just like the Director was able to choose between the Brown Zone or the Yellow Zone or the Grey Zone. Except that free will can sometimes be perverse. Like those people that believe they have made a good decision when choosing between options, the fish was also showing its discernment when refusing the hard, pink-coloured crumbs in favour of the sweet and softened ones. Regrettably, despite its choice – the unchosen path often runs to meet us – the refused crumbs would dissolve, filling the still water, and then the fish's gills, with their tranquillising properties.

The fish's heart stopped on the second morning of the little game. And, after licking the suede gloves, the Cat licked its own whiskers and rolled its eyes with contentment. That morning it had been served an unusual breakfast.

After which it slept, curled up on top of the refrigerator, for two consecutive days.

A Party speech (I): How to educate the people after disaster

With stomachs becalmed after countless canapés, it was now the hands of Party members doing the talking.

In the Government Tower applause rang out like a lion's roar.

Up on the ninth floor, in the ballroom, the one with the lustrous chandelier, the Bald Minister stood up and walked to the lectern as his name blared out of the speakers.

As the Bald Minister's suede shoes glided along the carpet, two enormous blue flags with the Government stars on them unfurled behind the stage. And the national anthem started playing loudly.

Party members, sitting at the tables, put down their wine glasses to get on their feet and give another use to their throats. Having hopped up the carpeted step, the Bald Minister acknowledged the ovation.

On stage, with speaking notes open in front of him – the speech he had dictated earlier, and which his Assistant had typed up – he ran his hands over the lectern top, and silence fell.

Dear friends.

(*The Bald Minister begins in a low voice, as if dragging the voice from the bowels of the earth.*)

It's very good to see you all. (*Pause.*) It really is. It's a joy to be here today in front of you all. (*Long applause; the beating of palms like heavy rain on a window; the Bald Minister's hands gesturing for the Party members' loud hands to quieten down.)* Thank you. I want to begin this speech by remembering that, since the fateful day in our history that this Government and our Party took upon themselves the benevolent task of rebuilding it from the ruins of the disaster, our City was methodically planned and designed. *(Pause.)* Cleansed and disinfected. *(Pause.)* Not only to seek urbanistic balance, or architectural grandeur, but also to achieve a fair organisation encompassing society *(pause)*, industry *(pause, looking to the left of the audience)*, the judiciary *(pause, looking to the middle of the audience)*, the army *(pause, looking to the right of the audience)*, business, leisure. And all using the full colour spectrum. *(Pause.)* It's true...I know...Educating the people is an arduous process, it takes time. People are unruly and unbiddable. And to expect to make all those wretches march in the same direction betrays either naivety or idealism. We learned this from the Great Disaster. You know that. *(Pause.)* This Government started from nothing. But from an organised and different kind of nothing. A nothing that springs from human guts. A nothing that understands and accepts natural differences: biological, organic, cellular. That is why our policies boldly exclude and separate. That is the truth. Don't you believe that it is stupid and hypocritical to aspire to equality? *(Some applause and shouts of: true! Here here!)* You know this. You know. *(Dramatic vocal inflection, and gradually rising voice.)* The poor and the beggars, the hungry and the sick, the crippled and the crazy, the garbage and the stray dogs, you know this, all that scum was swept off our streets by this Government's competent broom and left far away from here! Far beyond the Wall! Where their shouts and their bodily fluids cannot contaminate our social equity and our political hygiene! *(Thunderous applause, standing ovation, convulsive cheering. The Bald Minister uses this moment of high emotion to drink water and polish his pate with a towel. He waits for the applause to subside and continues.*) Yes, I know this, and you know this and much more. (*Pause.*) But there is something else. (*Pause, with eyes widening.*) And it is that something that I continue hearing as background noise, as a murmur, an evil dog-whistle of doubts and questions, resentments and fears, spurred on by the beast of dissatisfaction. (*Mournful pause with deep gaze that sweeps the audience: left, right, middle.*)

A Party speech (II): Do the people want to marry the bride? Or do they want horses that piss wine?

Some Party members I run into in our Tower's halls and lifts tell me: the people are dissatisfied. And I reply: they are dissatisfied, good for them. (*Pause, gesturing in resignation.*) They tell me we need new ideas, new policies. And I ask: new ideas, you say? New policies? And I add: certainly. And I ask again: but which? (*Short pause, followed by increased agitation.*) What, then, does this Party want? What, then, does this Government want? To govern boldly, or to listen to people's out-of-tune songs? To listen to the people singing B-sides? I ask you, then: what song do the people want to sing? What, then, do the people want? The people are a sumptuous chaos. Do they want to sing? Dance? Work? Eat? Drink? Sleep? Copulate? Yes, all of this, and more? If you have the answer, please, I beg you ... (*Long and uncomfortable silence with a puckered smile wrinkling the Bald Minister's mouth.*) Can any of you here tell me what the people really want? (*Short pause, eyes widening.*) Is it sirloin steaks in a cream sauce? (*Moderate laughter.*) Perhaps a not-so-white winter? (*Some guffaws.*) Maybe a sky filled with berries? Or horses that piss wine? (*Generalised laughter.*) Wait, wait, let me guess: THE PEOPLE WANT FREE-DOM. (*After stressing each syllable of the last word, the hubbub dies down, and silence falls on the audience as if at a wake.*) FREE-DOM, right? Of course: freedom. That virginal, chaste and beautiful bride. Forever faithful. And what do the people want to do with the bride? To marry her and jump over the Wall, like a storybook hero, carrying her in their arms? Or to have a lustful picnic in the Forest with her? Or perhaps the people need that bride to choose the best colour with which to paint their walls at home? But tell me, my friends . . . Could it be . . . Could it be that the bride . . . Pretty, desirable . . . Truly . . . Could she be a property? A conquest? Might that bride even be a choice? Like the freedom to say: don't die now, you mustn't; don't fall sick, I don't want you to. Or perhaps the freedom to say to one's heart: I don't want you to beat like that, or here, in this place, agreed? (*The Bald Minister points his index finger at the Party members.*) So, tell me! Where is that bride's father, so we may ask for her hand in marriage? What do the people want, after all? (*A silence pregnant with small noises: a shoe sole rubbing against the carpet, fingers cracking nervously, teeth grinding, dry gulping.*) Yes, my friends. It's not easy, I know. Not easy . . . Shall I tell you what the people want? My friends . . . The people . . . Want . . . The people . . . Want . . . (*Long pause.*)

A Party speech (III): The people will learn the song

. . . They don't know. (*After the short beat needed for the joke to sink in, the reaction: riotous laughter and applause.*) That's it: THEY DON'T KNOW. (*From this moment, the Bald Minister's rhetorical talent takes flight, in a crescendo of emotional notes, tonal variations and exalted gestures, towards a climactic ending, denying the Party members any opportunity to react.*)

My friends. This much I know: today the people demand one thing, tomorrow they will demand another. This is the immutable law that governs them. They are today what tomorrow they reject. And tomorrow they will be what they rejected yesterday. And whatever they reject tomorrow is what they wanted to be the day before yesterday. It's sumptuous chaos. There is no consistency in the people, no stability or permanence. And our Government's and our Party's proud role is this: to rise to the challenge of creating stability based on organisation. Imposing goals. Rules. Humility. Resignation. We needn't wait for an accident to appreciate life. I remember, on this subject, a famous writer's words. '*There is hope, of course. But it is not for us.*' Except that the people are stupid. They were not made to understand. They understand nothing. But they always have an opinion. A voice. A murmur. Something to say about things they know nothing about. And that isn't all: after the Great Disaster, who rebuilt this City? We did! Who put solid roofs over people's heads? Basic comforts? Who created employment? We did! Today, everyone has access to medical care, to leisure, to clean streets; we have organisation and safety; crime has diminished to lower numbers than ever! Everything the people demanded before. And who is responsible for this? Who should they thank for all of this? This Party! This Government! Yet, today, when they have what they demanded yesterday, they remain dissatisfied. The beast continues to shout. The malevolent murmur. The background noise. So, I say this: let the beast shout. Let it bark. Let it howl if it feels like it. Our Government and this Party will not give in to those needy howls; nor will we take a single step back in what we believe is the appropriate execution of a policy meant for the common good! And furthermore: architecture, method, organisation, cleansing, the army – they are all instruments in our orchestra! They are the music of our Party and our Government, providing the proper song for the people to learn. A modern song, based on principles we will never give up on! A song that the people will learn – they will learn to sing it – they will learn, believe me . . . No matter how long it takes! The people will learn the song! And the lyrics to the song are these:

This Government has made and will make a word into: law!

This Government has made and will make an idea into: concrete!

This Government has made and will make colours into: order!

This Government has made and will make pies into: growth!

This Government has used and will use the whistling of bullets to temporarily tarnish the ground!

The butterfly of grains

The Maid dips her fingers in the bowl and strokes the grains. She caresses the rice.

You cannot be aggressive towards the rice, her Mistress had once said, in a tone of voice she cannot forget.

Her employer, the Redhead, took very seriously everything to do with food. From the careful selection of ingredients to their rinsing, and including the slicing and chopping, the cooking times, the condiments and oils, nothing was insignificant or left to chance. The Maid found it difficult to take in so much information and so many instructions, but she wanted to believe that her Mistress's constant scolding and reprimanding were a form of affection. Even more, the Maid suspected that the obsession with food, the outbursts and the capricious behaviour, were the Redhead's way of showing love, her way of expressing concern for others.

Perhaps this interpretation owed too much to her thick glasses and weak eyesight. People with poor eyesight are more inclined to believe in goodness.

Regarding the rinsing of brown rice, the Redhead had said to her:

. . . no, no, no, not like that, you're doing it wrong. This isn't like an apple, or a pear, where you can rinse vigorously. Rice is delicate. Very delicate. It's the butterfly of grains. It cannot be rinsed under the hard jet of water from the tap, it has to be immersed. So, you have to put the rice (the butterfly) into a bowl with the same gentleness with which you would put a sleeping child into its bed. You have to pour the water, sweet and patient, from another container, little by little, as if in a Turkish bath, on the body of the rice (the butterfly). Meanwhile, your well-trained hand must affectionately stroke the grains (the butterfly's wings). In a harmonious atmosphere, in a calm silence. With no tensions furrowing your brow, or screams ringing in your ears. Because just like a faithful sponge, the rice (the butterfly) will absorb that bad energy and the related emotions. And we, as we chew it thirty times once cooked, instead of receiving its life-giving energy, end up swallowing the ugly product of our temperament. And, instead of getting rid of evil, we ingest it once again, and chew on it, and absorb it in a perfect cycle.

So spoke the Redhead Mistress.
So did the obedient Maid try to rinse the rice (the butterfly).

Soup time, with impertinent questions

The short-sighted Maid holds the spoon, expectantly.

The Child, hand on chin, looks at the floor. Distracted, he keeps a beat, giving one of the table legs tiny kicks. On top of the tablecloth, in a deep bowl, what separates them: the steaming mix, green and yellow. A puff of vapour rises from the plate and the spoon, blurring the Child's eyesight and steaming up the Maid's eyeglasses.

It's hot!

I'll blow on it.

What is it?

You know what it is.

Lentils.

Yes.

The Cat appears under the table. It sniffs the soles of the dangling feet. It licks the Child's toes as if they were biscuits. The Child laughs at the tickles and seeks out the short-sighted eyes of the Maid, lost behind the thick glass. The laughter is contagious and is carried far. The Maid also shows her teeth. She takes the opportunity to move the spoon towards the Child's happy mouth. The Child stops smiling. He swallows, reluctantly, the steaming food.

The Cat's hungry.

It's had its food.

The Cat doesn't like the lentil soup.

I'll make him something else.

I'd like to be a Cat.

Why?

So I wouldn't have to eat soup.

The Child releases a barrage of questions to avoid the next spoonful.

Are you going to die?

What kind of question is that?

You'll die, won't you?

Yes, some day. Open your mouth.

It's hot.

I'll blow on it some more.

The Maid's hand moves downwards. Empties the spoon's content. Scrapes the edge of the bowl. Moves upwards. She blows. The Child's mouth opens wide. The Maid can see his harelip and the fault line in his rows of teeth. The Child asks:

Have you eaten the pies?

Yes.

And do you like them?

I do.

They're made of meat, aren't they?

Yes.

Do you know what animal?

No.

I do.

Do you?

He has told me that some of them are made of our own meat.

Right . . . Come on . . . Mouth open.

The wolves attacked a man in the Forest, didn't they? I'm scared of wolves.

The Maid freezes. The spoon held aloft.

How did you know that?

He tells me.

He . . . Who is *He*?

He . . .

*

The Cat jumped onto the table. The Maid stood up. She shooed it away with a shout.

Mother hates Father and Father hates Mother.

You're talking nonsense.

It's true. They hate each other. They kiss quietly, but they never talk. They don't even hug me.

I'm sure they do when you're sleeping. That's why you don't see them.

Do you think?

Yes.

The Maid sits down again. She picks up the spoon, arranges her glasses, frowns. She puts her other hand against her breastbone.

Does it hurt?

It'll go away soon.

Is it your heart?

It is.

A doctor has already operated on your heart, right?

Yes.

Do you have a scar?

I do.

Me too. A doctor tried to fix my lip, here, do you see? I was born with a split lip. I also have a scar. Father was also born with a split lip, and he also has a scar. A doctor operated on him. Doctors always end up operating on us, don't they?

Sadly so.

Father and Mother hug, and then hug me while I sleep?

Yes. But don't say anything. This is just between you and me: our secret.

The Maid winks, runs a finger down the place where her scar is and picks the spoon up again.

Our secret?

Yes.

OK . . . Does it hurt there?

Yes, sometimes it hurts.

You're gonna to die, aren't you? *He* said so.

Yes . . . Come on now, be quiet and eat the soup.

OK . . . I'll eat . . . But are you gonna die?

Yes. One day . . .

And after you die, they'll take you to the Factory and they'll put you in the Bank, which is where they put the people who die, isn't it? Father promised to take me there one day. To visit Grandpa. He's in the Bank.

Come on, open your mouth. You're getting on my nerves!

And me? Will I die one day?

The Maid stops moving the spoon. Her pupils dilate. Her heartbeat is irregular. She does not want to contemplate it, but cannot avoid it: what will happen to the Child when the thing that has not yet happened finally happens?

Are you finished?

No . . .

Are you still giving me that?

I will . . . I will . . .

Soup doesn't matter as much as death, does it?

No. Now be quiet. And focus on the soup like you focus on the piano. OK?

OK.

After two more spoonfuls, the Child asks again:

Have you spoken to *Him*?

What?

Have you spoken to *Him*? *He* has a nice voice.

All right, that's enough. Be quiet for a while. You haven't stopped talking since you sat down.

I'll stop. But you know . . . I talk to *Him* . . . And you know what . . . ? *He* answers. *He* talks to me. In the daytime I just hear *Him*. I don't reply. But at night-time I talk to *Him*. Yesterday *He* told me not to eat soup. *He* hates it too.

The Maid sighs.

But soup is important, and it's good. It'll make you grow strong . . . To be a great pianist you need to eat your soup. Besides, if you don't eat it your mother will punish you.

And she'll also punish you . . .

That's right.

Mother is always talking about soup and rice and chewing . . .

It's because she loves you.

It's because she's stupid.

Don't say that.

Mother chews her food thirty times, and she makes me chew thirty times. She looks at my mouth and counts to thirty. One, two, three, four . . .

Fine . . . But don't say that.

But you don't count how many times I chew, do you?

No.

Do you like me?

I do.

And do you like my music?

You know I do. You have little golden fingers.

And I have a secret.

Do you?

Yes. Don't tell Father. Promise you won't tell? If you promise you won't tell, I'll tell you.

I promise. Now open your mouth.

The Child swallows another spoonful.

I don't play by myself.

What?

When I'm tied to the piano, *He* whispers the notes into my ear, the beat. It's easy. It's as if *He* entered my hands and my fingers were flying . . . And I stop . . .

Open your mouth and eat the soup!

Soup . . . It's always about the soup! Soup doesn't matter more than music . . .

Come on . . . Please . . . Just do this one thing for me. Otherwise, your Mother . . . With you and with me . . . Open up, come on. Good. Just four more spoonfuls.

Two.

Three.

He also hates it, you know? *He* hates soup and hates Mother and hates Father. *He* says *He*'ll get *His* revenge. Sometimes *He* talks like *He*'s the Devil.

Goodness! Come on . . . Just one more!

Last one?

Yes.

And if I eat it, will you tell me a nice story?

Nice?

Yes.

And what is a nice story for you?

A story that gives me nice dreams. And doesn't have wolves.

And that's what you want?

Yes.

To have dreams?

Uh huh.

But what about when you wake up from your dream?

You tell me another story that gives me nice dreams.

And what if I told you that there are no nice stories? Or scary stories? There is only one story that happens over and over again and that is neither nice nor scary. It's a *scary-nice* story.

Is it the only one you know?

It's the story my mother used to tell me.

Does it have wolves?

There are no stories without wolves.

And will it make me dream?

That's up to you.

OK, tell me that one then.

Fine, but first, open up one more time.

Gymnopédie VI

The Thoughts: A brief summary of the Bald Minister's most important sayings

Thoughts do not have colours. But let's suppose that everything a man thinks was tinged in a particular colour and then pulled out of his head like a firework. What would the colour of air be in our Cities? What would the sky look like above densely populated areas? Through that tinge, that aura, that smear lifting from heads, understanding of *the other* would be possible, visible even. We would have something to grab onto. We could read those clouds. And be able to say, depending on whether they were yellow, pink, green, blue, purple, orange, brown, grey, black, I know what you're thinking. I don't need you to speak to know if I should stay away or come close. The vast range of saintly or beastly thoughts would be painted onto the atmosphere and, more importantly, would be easily identifiable.

No mutilated stuffed bear

Nobody says: this is a child's room.

Facing north, with a small window looking out onto the Wall, the Son's room is a cramped place, and dark. Four square metres with the rickety bed and the pine bookshelf interrupting the polished shine of the wooden floor.

No wooden rocking horse. No mutilated stuffed bear. Or lead soldier with its bayonet at the ready, or toothless pirate with a spade, or punctured football, or scrambled jigsaw puzzle. No trace colour on the walls, no trace of imagination or messiness visible on any of the surfaces.

In its coldness, the Son's room imitates certain military barracks, where the only thing that matters is sleep, efficient rest.

Because life, the full and disorderly life with which a child inevitably fills any space it breathes in, like a wholesome hurricane – that life, unbridled, had not entered that room.

In the Son's room there is rigour, cleanliness.

Order, discipline, monotony.

The things that matter most in the secure development of a child's spine.

Dialogue with darkness: Where you hear the heart sewing

Paying strict attention to the clock, the Son goes to bed at eight or eight thirty every night. After the religiously observed lentil soup ritual, with the Maid walking ahead of him, he goes up seventeen steps, opens the door, puts on his pyjamas and turns out the light.

Order, discipline, monotony.

The Son goes to bed with no Father and no Mother. No one to scratch his back. No warm milk or biscuits in his stomach to nudge him into sleep.

As soon as he hears the doorknob's metallic click, the Son covers his head with the duvet. He closes his eyes and starts his dialogue with darkness. The Son makes the most of night-time to speak to the voice that lives in his head. He talks to it about his Father, about his Mother, about the Maid, about the Cat, the piano and the lentil soup. If Mother knew, she would punish him. But there, in that most intimate of hiding places, his Mother cannot enter.

The Son gathers the duvet over his head. And there he talks about his days and his fears. As if he were sharing the greatest of secrets. The familiar voice, like a whimsical wind of words, replies. In two distinct tones. One: benevolent. The other: harsh, austere. Sometimes it thunders. And it proposes punishment for those that deserve it: the Father, the Mother, the lentil soup. And then tears spring and remain poised, like a tightrope walker, in the Son's eyes. Not tears of sadness, but of happiness, at the prospect of punishment. And, controlling his emotions, just like he controls his fingers over the keyboard, the Son stops the tears from falling. When he feels them coming, he holds them back. He forces his eyes to swallow the tears just like a mouth swallows its spit. The tear ducts suck them back in, causing his eyelids to swell. Thus, the dark circles permanently around his eyes: the result of emotions contained, not released.

When the dialogue is over, the Son's sweat-covered head emerges from under the duvet. Mouth dry. Eyes courting the darkness. He lays on his left side, heart drumming with its childish beat. The Son's heart ticks like a sewing machine. The mattress, the sheets, the pillow. It was his Mother who one day told him: the heart is a sewing machine. It sews people together. With hands pressed against his ears, the Son grinds his teeth to stop the noise of the sewing. As long as he can hear his heart, he won't be able to sleep.

Finally, he pulls his heels into his flannel-covered buttocks, turns his trunk and lays on his right side. His eyes look out towards the Wall, the snow and the night spreading outside the window.

The Son can see the Wall, the snow and the night, but cannot hear them.

And in that visual silence the Son finds distraction and falls asleep, forgetting about the sewing of his heart.

The Son's winter's night dream

The piano is an old moss-covered tree trunk.

He shuts his eyes and touches the damp keys in the tree bark's cracks. Sound rises from the woody knots. A sad and melancholy melody but, even so, the wolf is smiling. Showing its canines with colossal self-satisfaction.

The cold burns and soon the Son's fingers start losing their natural nimbleness. The musical performance becomes woeful, he misses some notes. The wolf with its fine-tuned ears protests:

Better stop. Your technique is poor.

After hearing the wolf's encouragement to stop, and in an attempt to finish his performance, he concentrates so hard on his heart that his heartbeat increases, bringing blood rushing to the tips of his fingers. And so, he finishes on a perfect note.

The crow on its tree branch and the frog in its puddle applaud. He takes a bow. Only then does he notice the wolf's grave silence. The wolf's eyes had become bloodshot:

No. Nothing to be done. Perhaps you can write books. What you've played for me isn't enough. You'll never be a pianist.

And then – to the crow's and the frog's horror – in a sudden agile movement, the wolf jumps at him.

Watching a prostitute from the window: Hearing the catcalls

Snow is reflected in the Redhead's two-coloured eyes.

From the window she can see a part of the square and the facades of some of the surrounding buildings.

The snow covers both what is beautiful and what is ugly. It conceals the faults. Tireless snowflakes gather volume, heaping over each other in a mantle of dense powder.

The Redhead watches the bustle on the street outside.

Seven soldiers talk, smoke, laugh. Out-of-tune guffaws. They pass a bottle from one to the other. Standing against the Wall, they put the bottle to their lips and drain it of the liquid that makes them feverish. Courage.

The Dwarf Prostitute is walking from the main square and headed towards the Club. She takes a wide detour to avoid the soldiers. The Dwarf Prostitute is wearing a hat, a scarf and an overcoat. The soldiers recognise her shape and her shadow. They whistle. They catcall until the shape and the shadow are lost in the dark.

Like the soldiers, the Redhead knows what the Dwarf Prostitute does at the Club. What she gives, what she does with her thrusting hips. The Redhead tries but cannot avoid feeling knots in her stomach. The stain of envy colouring her face. The

Redhead feels rage towards that small woman. Of the use she puts her disproportionate body parts to. Of the rough hands that squeeze them and reshape them. Of the strangers' pricks, stiff and persistent, knocking at her door and flooding her. And, above all, of those catcalls.

The Redhead thinks of one word as she watches the Dwarf Prostitute disappear around the corner.

She says it out loud:

Whore.

The green eye is more critical

The Redhead draws shut the curtains with images of the moon in all its phases.

She opens the jewellery box on the chest of drawers. Inside, the rusted ring that she wore on her finger in happier times. She tries to put it on again. After squeezing the flesh – her finger had become thicker and shorter, like she had – she finally succeeds. She puts her hand out, as if offering it, hoping to see it sparkle. Nothing.

The Cat, curled up at the foot of the bed, licks its paws, its belly, its bottom. The Redhead puts her finger in her mouth and bites the metal. She covers the ring in her saliva. Pulls it off. Places it inside the jewellery box. Undresses.

The pleated skirt, the woollen jumper, the purple shirt, the black bra piled up on the floor like the pelts of dead animals. The Cat observes the Redhead undressing without changing its expression. When it sees her in her diminutive underpants, it loses interest and continues cleaning itself.

The Redhead shivers and puts on her robe. She ties the belt into a knot. She shakes her curls off her nape, and they cascade down her back. She thinks about her Son. She remembers the lesson. His fingers cannot fail now. Only thirty-three days to go before the recital. It has been a long time coming. There is still enough time and all will be well, she says to herself, uncertainly.

She walks up to the mirror. She studies the reflected figure with scientific rigour. The fine lips pout or tighten, echoing her expression, guiding her eyes as they carry out the scrutiny. Her right eye, the green one, glints more impatiently.

The Redhead's green eye is more critical than its sibling, the brown eye.

They are mine and always with me

With a movement of her torso, her breasts come to life. They jump and wiggle. With cupped hands, she pushes them up. Supports them. Weighs them. Handles them as she would handle fruit to verify its sweetness. They are firm. Ripe. A few lumps. They have not yet drooped. A few more years and they'll wither and fall. That is true. Unable to escape gravity, they will hang over the folds of the soft belly. For now, they are still pointing. Pointing forward. No longer upwards. A single hand is not sufficient to hold them.

Head leaning towards her right shoulder. Sideways glance. She massages her breasts.

The Redhead says:

They are mine and always with me.

No one will take them from me.

As she kneads them, the Redhead remembers the hands of the Blond Doctor examining them. Searching for nodules, lumps. And copping a feel. The Redhead let him do it. It felt good. Caresses. She was proud of her breasts. Pale and full. Mounds of nourishment.

The dark nipple on her right breast hardens. The Cat raises its head from between its legs. The freckled hand squeezes. The Cat meows. Instead of milk, a drop of blood. The Redhead smells the blood. It might not be anything. Surely something benign. We'll only know after we have the test results. That is what the Blond Doctor said.

She shakes her head, her unruly curls. She covers up her breasts. Fastens her robe. Looks at the bed. The Cat meows. She steps towards it. Scratches its tummy. Lifts the duvet and slips between the cool bedsheets. The Cat approaches. Jumps into the bed. Curls up by the Redhead. The Redhead closes her long-lashed eyes and mentally rehearses the following day's actions.

Hormones and ova prospecting

The piano lessons, choosing the weekly menu, shopping for food, managing the Maid's chores: all of these are, for the Redhead, unmissable tasks. They occupy a large part of her daily time and energy. They focus and direct her towards what she considers essential. And so, absorbed, distracted, she can keep at bay the tumult of emotions. The rollercoaster ride of hormonal disturbances. But there are two moments, every month, where the Redhead's discipline and reason succumb to the power of hormones and the strength of ova. And then, no rationality or focus apply; and the Redhead descends, like an unprotected miner, into the emotional mine where hormones and ova are prospecting, singing wildly.

Lying on her bed, ready to dream, the Redhead stretches out her right arm. She feels the unoccupied part of the bedsheets. She feels flannel wrinkles instead of skin. The Cat's warmth instead of the Director's. She groans. A bitter taste reaches her tongue.

He, the man, the Father, the Director, is locked up in his office. He sleeps, seated, on a blue velvet sofa. Six walls, three rooms and five metres down the hall from her. The Redhead cannot remember the last time they shared a viscous night. But pride prevents her from getting up and facing the cold hall to knock on the office door. She had been taught: it is up to the man to make the first move. It is up to the woman to wait.

And she waited, hurt, dry, stone-like.

Pride is a heavy sack to carry, filled with stones to be hurled and with unmet expectations. By bending our backs, we can carry it with some effort. Our certainties punctured, we walk up and down roads. We see off the hours, days, moons and suns, seasons, years, until our deaths. Better that than asking others for help – or putting the sack down on the floor – to avoid revealing our weakness.

The Redhead has already been carrying that heavy sack for too long, asking herself:

Why won't he come and help me?
    What happened to him?
    What did he let life do to him?
    When did he become tired of love?
    When did his patience run out?
    Why doesn't he make an effort?

Every passing day, whatever once united the Redhead and the Director seemed to wilt away, like a flower cut from a plant and put into a vase. And it had all started after *the loss*. When the Director started to use the suede gloves. And grew out his beard.

Fish to the hook

Both the lack of warmth and the verbal and physical aloofness were beginning to leave their marks. It was increasingly obvious in the Redhead's behaviour that the Director was not being assiduous in his role. He did not woo her. He did not pursue her, though it is in the nature of the male to seduce and incite the female. And the absence, the lack of communication, turned every day into heavy hatred and rage unleashed on everyone else at the smallest provocation. And that blaze of hatred also let off an arresting aroma, a perfume only picked up by noses in the know.

The episode with the Blond Doctor, at the Hospital, was one example. Adultery brushed the Redhead's shoulder. Adultery is to marriage as a fish is to the hook. It is a matter of time, and the right bait. And the Blond Doctor had a fisherman's persistence. And more: he had a knowledgeable nose.

Although she refused to acknowledge it explicitly, that was not the first time, and would not be the last, that the Redhead became aware of her desire for a man other than the one she had married. But awareness is one thing, and the physical flesh is another. Awareness can deceive; the flesh cannot. The flesh is always honest: eat or be eaten, kill or be killed.

The fact is that on exceptional occasions, in the physical presence of *others*, and under the influence of provocative overtures made by obscene hands under a table, or whispered lasciviously into her ear, the Redhead's blood would pulse in her groin, and a blind heat, a painful fever, would almost unfasten her vagina.

Gymnopédie VII

The Engine: A brief summary of the Bald Minister's most important sayings

Fear is the indispensable engine of civilisation.

A powerful agent that, well oiled, well tuned, well handled, will allow economic progress. Uncontrolled, this mover of masses can become an adversary. An enemy instead of a friend. A frightening explosive that will cause politics to slide towards muddy territories and jam all the gears. The Government must be aware of this. And analyse judiciously all of its components and variations: from the minor resentment to the great terror, from personal caution to generalised panic. It is necessary to examine them all, test them, put them into motion. Lubricate fear. Carry out experiments. Study it in workshops. To extract as much benefit from fear as we can. And to move fast. It has been proven beyond doubt: love is useless, it only causes delays, does not create profits. And it is, perhaps, the greatest adversary of good politics.

So it is that, before making any decision, and as a formal and pedagogical aid to its ideas, laws, statistics and charts, this Government must always recognise the value of fear.

What do people fear the most?

That should be the first question.

A room for dust: God on the tabletop

The office is not well ventilated. Only the Director has per-
mission, and the key, to enter and breathe in the dense air of
his den.

The Director is sitting at his desk. His head bent forward
with the weight of the questions:

What if the Messenger is right?

What if that map . . . ?

Who will the Redhead give it up to . . . ?

The desk lamp shines on the desktop: the hands uncovered, the
two parts of the roughly drawn map taped together, the unused
suede gloves, the empty lentil soup bowl. And in a corner, the
blue velvet sofa he sleeps on.

An old wall clock, once belonging to his father, ticks away at
the time and generates dust. It is because of the incessant grinding of the clock's hands that dust is born, that fluff flourishes.
Fine carpets of dust cover every surface, smother every nook,
mute every object. Visible on the floor are the overlapping footprints made by the soles of the Director's slippers over the past
few months. Footprints in the white dust, as if it were snow.

His father had been right:

Wherever there is a clock, there is also dust.

As we don't believe in God, at least we can believe in dust,
the Director thought to himself.

God, then, is that incorporeal and persistent thing that lands with boredom on the desktop, or on a shelf, or on a skirting board.

The Director abandons his thoughts. He hears the tick-tock behind his ears. He fixes his eyes on the map. The place is marked with a red X. Pondering the possibility of finding a *treasure*, his harelip breaks into a near-smile. He directs the overgrown fingernail of his middle finger towards his hairy belly. From his navel he extracts a little ball of fluff. The fluff that nested there, straight out of the clock's factory. The Director's navel had grown from the years of digging. And from the belly's gradual expansion. And as the navel grew in size, so did the ball of fluff. Flicked away by the Director's fingernail, the ball of fluff floats through the air and lands softly on one of the trails of dust.

The Director hears himself saying:

Wherever there is a navel, there is also fluff.

He strokes his beard. His eye's butterfly-fluttering. The weight on his bladder. If the Messenger is right, he must find and dig up that thing as soon as possible. The snow will start to melt as soon as the sun rises. And the cover that the frozen whiteness provides will be short-lived. The warm season is approaching. And whatever is there, the sun will be uncovering it in no time.

The Director gets up:

I have to go and piss a few drops. I no longer believe in streams.

The imperturbable lover

The Director refuses to use the bed. He would prefer to have a crick in the neck, or a crooked spine from sleeping seated on the blue velvet sofa, than to share his matrimonial bed with the Redhead. Not because of the bed itself, but because of his well-developed hatred of company. Despite which, every night, sitting on the blue velvet sofa, the Director yearns for the bed.

One of the most important existential relationships we establish in life is with that horizontal object: a piece of furniture to lie down on or sleep in, comprising a platform onto which a mattress is placed, covered in bedsheets and blankets, or quilts, depending on the season.

The bed is that horizontal, inert body that welcomes our weight. And it adapts. Every day it welcomes us with open arms and legs. With no complaint about our odours, our breath, our humours, our snoring, our incontinence, our coughs, our anxieties or our desires. Passively, it serves the mass of our bodies. Asking for nothing in return: rest, copulation, dreams, or a sleepless night.

The bed is an imperturbable lover. It accepts all bodies and moves from body to body without taking sides. And it never dies so that it can see us die. So that we die upon it. In life, in death, unlike in love, the bed knows what it is doing. It knows the place it occupies in our lives and the responsibility that comes with that. And it delivers, it delivers. It always delivers. It is with us in moments of calm and euphoria. It works while our bodies rest. And it recovers while the ones who use it make a living elsewhere.

It knows our flesh, our bones, our breath. It knows the precise angle and position of the forearm in relation to the torso. The hand that feels pins and needles. The cardinal point towards which our head points. The jumble of hair. The clicking of knees. The nightmare sweats. The rattling of the heart. Even when the occupiers, through lack of aptitude or continence, urinate or spray their smells or other inconvenient substances, the bed welcomes them. It absorbs them with uncommon compassion, as if they belonged to it.

The bed is the most faithful of lovers. And this commitment without the wedding band remains eternal until death us do part.

Thus did the Director expound on the bed, sitting uncomfortably on the blue velvet sofa.

He could not expound similarly on the Redhead.

The ticket in the wrong hands: A coincidence

After saddling up the horse, he mounts: pushing up on the stir-rup with the strength in his good leg.

Years earlier, his right leg had been injured. During a raid on rebels, a stray bullet had perforated his knee. His kneecap was turned to powder. He had been limping ever since. And when-ever he walks, with that lopsided walk, he regrets not having foreseen what the world would do to him.

His sentry post is only two blocks away from the Government Tower. Every day, at exactly 14:15, after a brisk salute in the stables, his uneven heels dig in and the clip-clop of his horse's hoofs replaces that of the horse and the soldier doing the rounds of the urban geometry before him.

Amid the leaden silence he moves proudly through the num-bered streets and avenues. Through the peerlessly thought-out spatial architecture. Feeling the power that the animal gives him. Reins in his hand and the Government's star on the sleeve of his raincoat.

Snow is melting fast ahead of the imminent changing of the season. The blanket of cloud, erroneously referred to as sky, is losing its thickness: it is the colour of war. A fugitive moon, the night's guard dog, is getting ready to bark, and to call the stars out into their proper constellations, as if countless electric switches were suddenly flicked on after a long winter during which the universe's fuse box was out of service.

Later, lit by the false brightness of lamp posts standing every twenty metres, the Lame Soldier and his horse arrive at the Wall.

As soon as it feels the tug on the reins, the horse hesitates. The kitchen light is on. It has been the custom, when doing his rounds, for the girl with the glasses to come and watch him from the window. But today she is late. The Factory's shrill siren, announcing the change of shift, confirms it.

He dismounts near some hedges and pats the horse's haunches three times. The horse pulls its ears back and snorts. The Lame Soldier looks towards the window again, hoping to see the face with glasses. Nothing. He unbuttons his raincoat's pocket and pulls out a note. He unfolds it, rereads it. No spelling mistakes. The horse shakes its head and neighs.

Yes, you're right, I'll do it, says the Lame Soldier.

He opens the gate. He climbs the four steps with a lopsided gait. As if one of his shoulders were carrying the weight of more bones. His *soothsaying leg* tingles, gives him a signal. Something is coming. He approaches the window cautiously to look through it. Inside the kitchen, the Cat, in two movements, jumps from the floor onto the stool. And from the stool onto the window ledge. The Lame Soldier recoils instinctively, gun in hand. The note falls to the ground. His finger finds the trigger. He points the gun at the apparition. Then he laughs. The Cat nudges the steamed-up window with its head, purring. The Lame Soldier picks up the note and puts his hand against the glass, as if to caress the Cat.

You will be my messenger, he murmurs.

The Cat meows, eyes wide open, as if it understood. And in an acrobatic motion it disappears from sight. The Lame Soldier stands on his toes and peers into the kitchen: on the bench he sees a tray laden with muffins. He checks the window latches. He forces one of them open. He slips the note through the crack.

He turns away. Descends the four steps. Closes the gate. Raises his *soothsaying leg* and climbs onto the saddle. He grabs the reins.

Maybe the girl with the thick glasses will see the note, he says to the horse.

I'll wait for you at the stables

She reads:
Tonight. I'll wait for you at the stables.

The chords reached her from the living room. The lesson continued, with the Son tethered to the piano rehearsing his agile fingers on the keyboard.

The Redhead read and reread the note. She ironed out the words. Front, back, seams. Succumbing to a primate thought, she feels the fire flooding into her face. For a moment, there is no distinction between the colour of her hair and her blushing skin. She pushes the thoughts away. And the face returns to its natural pallor.

Tonight. I'll wait for you at the stables.
　　Yes, that was it. The paper was wet, some letters had run, the handwriting was crooked. But that was it. The Redhead looked through the window. Under the weak light she could just make out in the mud the Lame Soldier's fresh footsteps.
　　The imprint of the left boot was clearer, deeper.
　　Boots reveal the man who wears them.
　　The Cat meowed, persistent, at the Redhead's feet, expecting a reward. He had been a good messenger. The Redhead crumpled the note. She put it in her handbag. She picked up a ginger muffin. Nibbled it. Dropped some crumbs. The Cat licked the

crumbs with hygienic precision. Its rough tongue was like a hurried mop. The Redhead nibbled. Put her hand back in her handbag. Her mind was a whirlwind of conflicting thoughts. She read the note again.

Tonight. I'll wait for you at the stables.

The Redhead knew: the Lame Soldier was doing his rounds of the Blue Zone. She had crossed paths with him a few times. Those times, she had felt the weight of his admiring eyes on her body. The hungry gaze of someone who has no clean thoughts. The self-assurance with which certain pretty women are looked at. And she liked being looked at like that. A woman needs to be looked at forcefully. But she always suspected that, if there were any attraction at all, it might be between the Lame Soldier and the Maid. She had once caught them together, drinking tea at the kitchen table, and he had blurted out an excuse: he had brought her some firewood.

That day, the Redhead had chosen to believe the lie, knowing that she was being lied to. Yes, there was something in the air, and the exciting smell of ginger might be a sign. But what if, what if . . . that boldness was meant for her?

It's all a matter of smells

The Redhead thought the Lame Soldier was handsome, strapping, despite his defective leg. He had considerable physical strength, courage. And besides, when he was riding his tall horse, his physical defect was not visible. The horse made him more powerful. Most of the time he moved through the streets not with his unbalanced walk, but with his horse's elegant trot. And, armed, he viewed everyone from high up. Admiring the tops of people's heads.

What had made her uncomfortable, that time in the kitchen, when their shoulders brushed, was his particular smell. The Redhead's sensitive sense of smell detected an invisible film surrounding him and clinging to his uniform, or his skin, like an insidious disease. The Lame Soldier's smell was as strong or stronger than his horse's. Perhaps it was because of his constant proximity with the animal; the fact that his skin, like blotting paper, absorbed everything around it. But, for a sensitive nose more used to fine fragrances, that smell was almost an aggression. A trespass on the private property that was the Redhead's body. No one has the right to overwhelm another's sense of smell, whether through carelessness or through deliberate obscenity, or to intrude upon their body, the Redhead thought to herself.

As if that were not enough, the wagging tongues of women said that the Lame Soldier was endowed not only with strength and courage, but with an enormous penis, a penis like a horse, the colour of mud, which through lack of modesty or any sense of propriety he often pulled out, between four walls, under the light of the lamps.

The Cat meowed. The second movement was over.

With her head in a tizzy, ankles trembling, the Redhead took four bites of a ginger muffin. And she swallowed the mouthfuls without chewing the requisite thirty times.

She sprinkled the remaining crumbs over the floor.

The Director's winter's night dream

The night is as thick as lard. Dense like the Forest canopy. The sky is indistinguishable from the branches, darkness is indistinguishable from the foliage. No stars or moon.

The bear is three paces away. Lying on its side, it breathes noisily.

The Director, hands in his pockets, stares at it. Only a few metres from his potential death. He does not hesitate.

The bear awakens from its torpor, it raises an eyelid as it stretches its muscles in a spasm of sloth.

The Director comes close.

He senses for the first time the hot smell of the untameable, of what is beyond human, what devours mercilessly.

The Director is cold. He curls up by the hairy belly. He puts his head close to the animal's chest. He can hear the powerful beat of its carnivorous heart. He feels the safety and comfort of an offspring.

An eye regards him with no pity.

He senses that the bear is getting ready to leave.

Don't go. Not yet. I have something for you.

And out of his pocket he pulls a handkerchief. Wrapped inside the handkerchief, which he unfolds carefully, are four severed fingers. Blue. In a good state of conservation. He offers them to the bear.

Are you hungry? You can eat them. I found them on the Forest floor. I don't know who they belong to. You know that my Son is a pianist? He's still learning. He takes lessons. But these are of no use to him. They are too thick. I don't know who they belong to. A good pianist needs thin, long fingers. These are of no use to him.

The bear approaches with drool dripping from its mouth. It gobbles up the blue fingers without hurting him. It licks the palm of his hand, then turns on its hind legs and walks away, into the lardy darkness.

The wish to hide the aberration:
Preparations

Placed on his legs, the gloves.

They are the fine curtain separating the hands from the rest of the world. At a bad moment of his life, the Director's hands had lost their weight, their bones.

The Director covers his hands: the gloves are still the possible refuge from external aggressions. But there is, also, the wish to hide them. The Director does not dare to leave home and expose his incomplete hands to strangers' eyes.

Sitting on the garnet-coloured velvet sofa, the Director looks at the clock. According to his estimates, he should be back in three hours, and no one will have noticed his absence. There is no place for miscalculations. The second half of the map, which the Messenger gave him after they reached their agreement, shows the exact location of the *treasure*, and the route to get there.

The Director's heart cannot hide its excitement about the prospect of recovery. As a precautionary measure, and to avoid any mistakes caused by an overexcited heart, he lets two tablets melt under his tongue. There, safer like that.

He pulls the torch out of the knapsack. He tries to open the small orifice at the base of the metallic cylinder. He is unable to. He lays the torch down on the desk. He takes off his left glove. He holds the torch with his gloved hand and uses the fingernail of his ring finger to open the torch's battery compartment. The old batteries slide out. He replaces them with new batteries as if he were putting bullets into the cylinder of a revolver that is ready to be fired. If only he could fire a gun. But the wooden prosthetic fingers he slides into the gloves are an artifice. With no thumb, he might be able to fill the cylinder, but not to cock the gun. Make it click.

Who knows, maybe soon . . . ?

Having confirmed that the torch works, he shuts the chamber. He straps the knapsack onto his back. He turns off the lamp. He remains standing, immobile, attentive to any noise, until his eyes get accustomed to the dark.

The silence is unassailable. The house sleeps. He opens the door.

When the Director thinks he is on the inside, despite being on the outside

The Director counts sixty seconds. He takes nine steps and stops outside the Redhead's door. He puts his ear to the wooden door. Nothing. She must be in the land of dreams, in the embrace of dark calm.

As always happens when he walks past the Redhead's door, a part of him thinks:

Knock.
   Knock and make her get up.
   Make her open the door.
   Enter.
   Embrace her and make love to her.
   Beg for her forgiveness.
   Open your heart.

But then, the voice moves away, just as the Director now does, taking long strides.

When it comes to people, everyone is on the outside. Even when they believe themselves to be on the inside. What to do if the heart hides behind the rib cage and no one can see it? Hopes, imagination, sweet words and promises are all nice, but not reliable. Not even a closed door is an impenetrable defence. One shove, one kick, and the wood, the lock, can give way. But even with the kick, the shove, the damaged wood, are we really through the door? Yes, we are in. But are we actually inside? No. We are always on the outside. The fact is: the Redhead is not on the other side of the door, dreaming, as the Director imagines her to be. Like the Director, the Redhead has made the most of the night to recover something she had lost. The Redhead is not inside, as the Director thinks, but outside. That is all there is to it.

But are we ourselves not always too busy pointlessly trying to find explanations when everything is unknowable? When we are always on the outside? And what else can we do but shrug our shoulders and carry on with our hands empty of all certainties?

Onwards.

The Director walks down the seventeen steps in his socks. His boots are on the kitchen floor. He pulls up a chair. Sits down. He opens the refrigerator door, so that the feeble light helps him with his task. He pulls on the boots using his good fingers as pincers: the tips of his middle fingers pressing against the fingernails of the index fingers. Then, the muffled sound of a jump. The Cat yawns as it stares at the Director. It stretches. It sneaks between the legs and purrs like an engine. The Cat's eyes move like a pendulum, oscillating between the refrigerator, from where it is getting a cocktail of smells, to observing with unique sensitivity the extraordinary gymnastics performed by those dark-skinned fingers. The Director stands up. And before closing the refrigerator door, sensing the start of an impending meow, which amid the silence might have worked as an alarm, the Director takes out milk and pours some into a bowl.

As soon as the Director's excited boots were pushing down on the bicycle pedals, the Cat, sitting outside, rubbed its whiskers with its front paws. And with its sandpapery tongue, it licked its back paws, its belly, its sex.

Private treasure

Forty-sixth day after the Messenger's arrest.

Guided by the torch's beam of light, the Director breathes with the complicit thrill of return. The worry and the excitement of the rescue operation were now over. Once again, the Messenger had been right. God's words, or the Messenger's premonitory dreams, or the omens, or who knew what else, had led the Director to a happy reunion.

He is carrying them on his back, inside a box in his knapsack. And soon he will be putting them inside the icebox. Four of them. Blue and intact. He had found them. Now they were his. Four.

To find is not to steal, and whoever finds something first owns it. Wolves and bears had failed to sniff them out.

Even so, the recovery of that *treasure* had not been without its hiccups. The difficulty was not in finding its horizontal location, but instead finding its vertical one, its depth. It took him many minutes, kneeling on the ground, digging up the snow. As if that were not enough, he could hear the wolves howling their arias in the distance, and had begun to feel like a hare. But proximity to danger has one advantage: it makes us feel more alert and alive than we did before the threat. The howls gave the Director an enhanced sense of urgency: they catapulted his haste.

He walks around the edge of the frozen lake. Fir trees line the path, surrounding the icy mirror. A row of gigantic tibias and fibulas, unfractured and arranged with military precision, protects a trench. The sharp easterly wind charges like a trapped bull. The cold air is playing tricks: it stings his lungs with no warning, and then comes out of his mouth like a thick cloud: a biological illusion.

The Director scrutinises with some difficulty the landscape stretching out to the south. His eyes hurt. His anorak's hood hangs limply. The sharp pain in his lower abdomen is a warning: time to stop. But the Director cannot stop. He has another fifteen minutes to go. Until he reaches his bicycle.

The bastard child of a sideways thought

He has left the gigantic tibias and fibulas behind.

The number 48 boots get stuck in the snow. The torch's trembling beam barely lights up the thirty frozen centimetres ahead of the Director's next step. The Director no longer feels the gloved fingers of the hand holding the torch. His prosthetic fingers are coping better than the ones filled with blood. No cold can get into those false bones.

He switches the hand that is holding the torch. And as he does so, for no apparent reason – perhaps the unexpected happiness of having found what he sought? – and emerging from who knows what part of his subconscious, comes an image. An instant of pure past. A perverted mental photograph taken fifteen years earlier. Right after a good fuck. The Director had cracked the bathroom door open. The Redhead, naked, sitting on the toilet: traces of her recent orgasm still on display in her youthful smile, her cunt dripping with fresh semen, hands pressed together between her knees, painted toenails pointing at the ceiling, heels pointing outwards, toes inwards. Then, the unguarded sound of a stream of urine splashing the ceramic. Warm liquid gold colouring the cold white toilet bowl. The tenuous steam produced by the clash of temperatures. A flash of red, the pubic thatch trimmed back to the groin's creases. And the folding of toilet paper into three. Rounded breasts hanging as the trunk leans forward. The forearm moving back and forth with the cupped hand behind the buttocks.

Fifteen years ago. A time when the doors between the Director and the Redhead were not shut. A time when the Son was no more than a hypothetical sperm that might one day win the race. A time of beautiful, complete hands. A time of nurturing affections and abundant words. A time when the firmness of the Redhead's skin defied gravity. A time when the Redhead welcomed the Director's gaze into her most intimate places. A time when the Director's penis filled with blood at the smallest provocation. A time when pissing meant releasing a stream. A time when all of this – pissing, fucking, eating, gazing, talking – was pleasurable. No tomorrow, no yesterday. That was it.

The Director did not know where this memory had been hiding. Remembering is not easy. The past is corrupted, and memory brings us closer to melancholy. Perhaps at some other time this had been an arousing memory. Not now. Not after the recovery of his *treasure*. The strange thing was that such a sepia-tinted memory did not involve the *good fuck* itself. No matter how hard he tried, the Director could not remember the positions they had tried. Or the movements they had made. Or the arena in which their tongues had mingled. Or the words exchanged: neither before, nor after. He could not even recall the taste of saliva in his mouth from a kiss that might have led to all the rest. He could only remember the aftermath. Post-coital. The position on the toilet. The freckled face glowing with a different smile. The smell, both sweet and pungent, of the urine streaming out of her and into the network of sewers.

Perhaps it was the pain in his frostbitten fingers that brought on the memory, or the persistent need to urinate. The Director had read somewhere that it is common for *the bastard children of sideways thoughts* to flow into people's minds in winter. The time of darkness is when the unexpected consequences of muzzled desires come to life. Because the winter is a time of inward thinking. The cold forces us to look inside ourselves. When the sun escapes, it lights a candle within. And all our pores shut down to prevent the light, weak as it is, from escaping.

The truth is that, since recovering his *treasure*, the Director would have given everything, absolutely everything, to celebrate by pissing properly. To feel the force of the hot stream of freshly filtered piss. He even thought about pulling off his gloves and giving it a try. But better not to, with that cold.

He still had a five-minute walk ahead of him.

Morse code: And what if a God was behind this?

Four drops.

A tiny dribble.

Three more drops.

Two more drops, with effort.

And another tiny dribble.

What a relief. This was promising.

Looking proudly into the toilet, the Director said:

At least I can piss in morse code.

He plugged the bath plughole. He opened both taps at maximum pressure. He used his feet as a thermometer and corrected the temperature. His toes wriggled as he plunged them into water. He raised his left arm and sniffed his armpit.

The Redhead had once told him:

A man's smell matters a great deal.

There is no doubt: tonight, the Redhead is like a clot in the Director's brain, threatening to cause a stroke. The Director shakes his head, hoping to get rid of it.

Why does a man's smell matter?

Why does the Redhead insist on making him feel uncomfortable?

Earlier it was the dirty image in his mind, now it's her words about human biology?

And must it be precisely tonight?

He ungloves his hands using his teeth. He shuts the taps, pulls in his knees, lets his body sink. His flaccid penis, bobbing like seaweed in the wavelets caused by his immersion. He allows himself to remain in that watery comfort for ten minutes. Softening like butter in a bain-marie.

He gets out of the bath, dripping. Opens the third drawer in the chest. Among the jars of tablets and pomade tubes he finds the pack of cigarettes. He picks up the lighter using the index, middle and ring fingers of his left hand. With a triumphant gesture, he uses his right hand's middle finger to turn the metal spark wheel. The flint releases a spark. The mouth fills with smoke.

He returns to the bath with the cigarette, caught in a smile. A smoke to celebrate a good night. It had been a long time since the Director had enjoyed one so much. He sinks into the water and looks at his hands. And he does not call them *claws* or *pincers*. It is the first time, since *the loss*, that he does not feel sadness or shame, the melancholy of loss. Now he has them. Four of them. Not there, where they are missing. But kept in a box inside a refrigerator.

Who knows, maybe soon . . .

The Messenger had once again been right. And the Director was slowly beginning to yield to the evidence of his powers.

What kind of man is that?

And what if there really is a God behind all of it?

And what if the Messenger's dreams are short cuts to what will come?

After considering these hypotheticals, he was once again struck by a question that made his feeling of wellbeing disappear and made him swallow hard.

Has the Redhead already given it up?

The Redhead dreams of the change of season

Everything begins with larvae. And ends with larvae. In a garden seeded with larvae.

The great female is speaking, reclining on a tuft of dry grass.

Eighteen black and hairy legs. One and a half metres in length. Weighing ninety kilos.

The great female continues:

To get where I am, I had to devour thousands who, like me, aspired to the highest position. I devoured my sisters. My entire family, and others not related to me. I don't regret any of it.

The Redhead looks around.

Around her, within a radius of five or perhaps six kilometres, the landscape is all yellow.

And the further she gazes, the yellower and wider it looks. It could be sunflowers. Or wheat, or barley, but it is not. They are cicadas. Billions of male cicadas singing to the sun. The song of the males is devastating, torrid. A machine-like sound, deafening, growing in intensity every time the queen's voice is heard.

The Redhead perspires as she looks at the queen, who continues:

It is in what is invisible, and not in what is visible, that life corrupts and dances. That is why we must sing. These males you see here have hibernated for years. Now they are awake and singing for me. War is on its way, and it is necessary to procreate. All of them will mate with me, and I will generate offspring from all of them. After they mate with me, I will eat them. From that, more larvae will be born, and even more larvae that will devour each other before the next battle. And I will remain here, in expectation, to generate life and to feed off it. I am the great mother. The beginning and the end are in my abdomen.

After the speech is done, the Redhead walks away from the queen. And as she walks away, the ground crunches beneath her feet. Her bare soles press down on crackling carapaces. Insects crying out.

The males are preparing to mate with the queen.

The singing increases in volume.

There is no clear space on the ground.

Everything is yellow, and everything that is yellow sings.

SUMMER RECITAL

Gymnopédie VIII

The Music (II): A brief summary of the Bald Minister's most important sayings

Everyone knows because everyone has experienced it. And it needs to be understood: music enchants easily. It breaks through the heart's defences, or poisons the guard dog of reason, to rob us of what is most intimate and bring pools of soulful tears to our eyes. But worse: music, when executed with evil intent, can awaken inappropriate emotions, empty our minds. It makes us believe in something that is not here, before our eyes. So, the radios playing in our own homes, day and night, become an open tap contaminated by miracles, releasing water that is dangerous for public health. It is this Government's duty to purify that stream, or stop the flow of water, for good.

We must be courageous.

This Government will legislate music.

The hand sliding over the shoulder:
It's our baby

The sun was rising. Two soldiers smoked and played cards in the sentry box at the border. A couple approached from the square in the Yellow Zone. The mother pushing the pram and the father with his hand on her shoulder. A sliver of sunlight danced on the Wall, confident in its progress. The wind had changed direction, and the air was filled with the scent of incineration and pastries.

The mother's eyes were damp. Worry and tiredness had accumulated in her face. Every now and then she leaned over and stuck her head into the pram. The father waited for the soldiers to arrive, his gaze lost on the barbed wire. His hand on his wife's shoulder.

The bald soldier, without his beret, played his winning ace, stubbed out his cigarette and gathered the pies on the table. With a smile on his face, he said to the other:

You lose. It's your turn.

The Blue-eyed Soldier left the sentry box, cigarette dangling between his lips, gun strap slung over his shoulder. Cigarette smoke, blown about by the wind, getting in his eyes. He dropped the cigarette onto the pavement, and put it out with his boot. He squatted, picked up the cigarette stub and put it into his pocket. He approached the barrier. He looked over at the woman pushing the pram.

You're up early.

Good morning, officer.

What's the matter?

It's our baby, the mother said hurriedly.

The father squeezed her shoulder. It was for him to explain.

Yes, it's our baby, officer. He was feverish all night. The syrup we gave him is not working. And in our Zone's pharmacy there are no more medicines.

Your pass?

Yes . . . The thing is . . . I mean . . . We wanted to ask you a favour . . . It's for our baby . . . He has a high fever . . . And in the Blue Zone there are other medicines. What I mean is . . . It won't take us long to get there and come back.

Your pass, the Blue-eyed Soldier repeated, smiling at the mother. He pushed the coloured ribbons dangling from his beret behind his shoulder, as if they were long hair.

The baby was about to start crying.

The mother leaned over. The soldier stared at her breasts. The tears started.

Officer, it's my baby. He's . . .

The father squeezed her shoulder firmly. The mother became quiet. The soldier ran a finger over his gun.

I can see it. And I'm sorry. But you know the rules. No stamped pass, no joy. I'm just following orders, you understand? The Government makes the rules.

It won't take us long to go there and back. If you want, or if you allow, I'll go on my own. I mean I'll hurry over and come back in a minute. While my wife stays here and looks after the baby. Officer, we're not from the Brown Zone. We're from the Yellow Zone.

Silence.

The soldier sighed. He looked in the other direction. He gazed at the sliver of sun rising slowly above the Wall to reveal itself in full. He fondled his weapon. And said, addressing the mother:

Wait here. I'll speak to my superior officer.

The father squeezed the mother's shoulder, unable to contain his smile.

The mother rested her head on the father's shoulder.

They watched the soldier go into the sentry box.

They smiled at one another.

The father said:

All will be well, you'll see.

The Blue-eyed Soldier came back, a newly lit cigarette between his lips.

Here's what we're doing. I spoke to my superior and we'll make an exception. It's about a baby, after all. But we're sticking our necks out here. Life is long for some, though for some stupid people it can be too short. D'you know what I mean? So, here's what we'll do: you, sir, will go with the baby and come back. And while you do whatever you have to do, madam – and he pointed at the mother's full breasts with the barrel of his rifle – will wait for you, there, inside our little hut.

The father's hand slipped off the mother's shoulder. His eyes lowered.

The mother took the hand before it shattered like a vase falling on the floor. And she squeezed it with the same firmness with which he had previously squeezed her shoulder. The mother knew it was pointless to put up a fight. And that some choices need to be made.

She said:

Yes. It's our baby. You go, buy it and come back. Bring the medicine. And all will be well.

The soldier with eyes blue like a deep river lifted the barrier.

The sun moves across the sky, and everyone wants to be (I)

The sun spits light, heat. The snow melts.

The obstructive clouds are now hurtling towards the mountains in the north and beyond.

Dragging with them the darkness, the silence.

With the arrival of summer, windows across the City are open to let in the air. Curtains are drawn. Dust is shaken off blankets and bedspreads. Light clothes, long buried, are pulled from the bottom of drawers. Mattresses are turned over. Pillows are hung out in the sun.

Men start sweating abundantly as soon as they wake up. Women, meanwhile, do so delicately. Armpits become sticky, and smelly. Groins slither. The thirst begins. And the giddiness.

Later, the men tighten their belt buckles again, the women let their skirts drop back down.

After doing it, they go out.

On the streets, the sun beats down on the soft skins, the scalps. The caramel sun impels them to use hats, or to place hands over brows to be able to see. It reminds them of everything they had forgotten during the winter. Men and women, and the children already playing on the streets with balls and pebbles, look up. And not just at the Tower. Not just at the Factory's two chimneys. Finally, there is some sky. A kind of blue freedom. And at night, stars and constellations. With no interference from the clouds beyond the concrete horizon.

In the City, men and women and children appear in large numbers.

And they are still not satisfied: they want to continue being.

The metamorphosis: The beard and the fly

Because it is in the nature of some internal transformations to also express themselves externally, that morning, when he looked in the mirror, the Director decided to shave off his beard. Or rather, to ask the Maid to do it for him. After so many years with his face hidden, so many years with his face camouflaged, the Director hardly recognised himself.

After the Maid had wiped away the remaining shaving foam with a towel, he asked himself: that man there? Is it me? He confirmed: yes, it's me, but with a lighter soul.

Ever since he had recovered his *treasure,* he had felt more confident and relaxed. Even the little squirts of piss had returned. God bless those little squirts! And the challenges that life, so crafty and long in tooth, had thrown at him no longer felt so insurmountable. He had the legs to deal with them. What were those challenges, after all, other than cardboard boxes – some very heavy, others empty – that he could kick up into the winds?

And what mattered most was this: to kick up the right boxes, with no fear of what they might hold, with no fear of smashing his toe.

However, there remained a *fly* in the ointment of the Director's new and refreshing state of mind. Whenever we gaze with satisfaction at a landscape, there is always a *fly* to interrupt our delight. And this *redhead fly* was still buzzing around. Driving him to distraction. As if the Director's mind were an irresistible sugar cube, or (because flies are not very picky about their choices) an appetising and fresh heap of cow dung.

Because he did not have the necessary insect killer to dispatch this highly resistant insect, the Director decided that he would shortly pay the wise Messenger another visit in his cell. So that he might shed light on the right steps to be taken.

The Tower and the Redhead

The grass grows green, pushing through the weight of the soil, only to become yellow beneath the weight of the sun.

The sun takes over the Forest, the City.

The Government Tower's heavy shadow falls on rooftops, borders, facades, pavements. It falls on the Wall. It falls on the lava-coloured hair of the Director's wife as she makes her way through the Blue Zone in high heels.

Click-clack click-clack.

Trotting elegantly on the pavement.

Competing with horses.

There are false rose bushes growing like ivy on top of the Wall. Unruly bushes of barbed wire that cut and cause to bleed anyone who touches them. Tangles of sterile stems and thorns that produce no roses. The grey thorns produce only blood.

The Government Tower is the tallest building in the City. Its shadow moves over every part of the City like a giant and protective finger. It is the human finger, raised, that points. Announcing to everyone where the power lies.

The Redhead slows the click-clacking of her high heels. She walks beneath the shadow of the Tower. She feels as if she were beneath an apple tree: on tiptoes, her heels raised, longing for the rosiest apples hanging from a high branch.

Like anyone who is human, the Redhead wants to be what she is not, to have what she does not have. Her desires vary with the days and the moons. Today, for instance, the Redhead glances at the Tower as if she were glancing at an elegant, charming man. But there are other days, though not many, when she sees red only from hearing the words *Government* or *Minister* or *Pies*.

But today, the Redhead wants to make the walls of the Tower her own.

Within those walls there is no dust, and the temperature is evenly comfortable year-round.

That is what the Redhead believes and what she dreams of: to wake one morning and not see the dust that settled on the dining table, to be able to sit at a window from which she can see far away.

The Redhead stretches her perfumed, swan-like neck, and focuses her attention on one of the sixth-floor windows. She harbours the intimate hope that some member of the Government might be observing her from behind that window. She will never know whether, at that precise moment, someone is watching. This uncertainty makes her smile, bite her lip, adjust her skirt.

Her mouth and fingernails are painted cherry red. Her earlobes pierced by fantasy earrings. She amuses herself by twisting one of her many curls around her deliberate finger, pretending she is doing it distractedly. Beneath the hem of her skirt, her calves are depilated.

As she looks up at the sixth-floor window, in a constant to-and-fro of thoughts and desires, the Redhead imagines the Director, on the other side of the glass, beckoning with his suede gloves. And her two-toned gaze is ignited with the ardour of a wicked female.

For a long time, the Redhead has been carrying the heavy weight of rage. And, from time to time, a residue of that rage surfaces. The Redhead's rage, like so many other things she pushes back down, appears to be dormant. But that appearance is deceitful. The Redhead's rage is like the toxic waste we hide beneath a blanket of earth to put it to sleep, with the vain hope that time and depth will eventually do the work for us.

He turned down the Bald Minister's invitation to be part of the Government, the Redhead says.

And he doesn't care about his Son's education. He is a weak man, and a sad one. A coward who avoids conflict. And if he doesn't have the fingers needed to govern, to put up a fight, he clearly doesn't have the fingers to make me wet. If he didn't use those wretched gloves, the ears in these walls might be getting an earful.

The Redhead knows that it is only because of her Son that she can expect to go up into the Tower. The Son has capable fingers. It will be because of her Son's fingers that the Redhead will finally be able to climb into the lift. When the summer recital takes place, she will finally find herself in the ballroom with the lustrous chandelier.

The Redhead wants the apple

Every morning the Bald Minister looks out the window. But, like the Gods, he never allows himself to be seen. Smoked glass covers part of the Tower's facade. It thwarts transparency: the glimpse of a face or of the movements made by someone who is chewing. The Tower's darkened windows quash any external curiosity. Allowing only those on the inside to engage in continuous vigilance and, perhaps, even punishment.

The Bald Minister fondles the apple while he watches the Redhead looking up from the middle of the square, hiding in the Tower's shadow. The persistent rubbing of the apple smooths the linen of his trouser leg. The Bald Minister puts the apple in his mouth. The hard apple groans and squeaks. The Bald Minister's teeth chew the apple while his eyes look violently at the Redhead.

He says:

The Redhead wants the apple and doesn't know how to get it. She can't climb this tree.

The Bald Minister, contented, eats the apple core.

He burps loudly and rubs his sticky hands.

Down below, the Redhead moves out of the Tower's shadow.

She hurries home.

She feels an irrepressible itch somewhere that she should not.

Womanly blackberry juice

The Secretary with brown eyes and black eyeliner comes into the Bald Minister's office carrying a bowl of wild berries on a silver tray.

The Bald Minister orders her to sit on the sofa.

The ritual of the blackberries is about to begin.

Every year the Bald Minister shudders with excitement at the arrival of summer and blackberries. The Secretary knows what to do: seated on the sofa, she pats down her skirt and, with deliberate slowness, enhancing the eroticism, opens her mouth and places five blackberries onto the moist carpet of her tongue. Deep purple on porous red, times five.

While the blackberries are being moved from bowl to tongue, the Bald Minister, on his knees on the carpet, his restrained hands on the Secretary's knees, watches the open mouth with a dentist's keenness. He likes to see the back teeth: blackened and decaying molars. The Secretary's mouth is not in full health, adding more excitement to the ritual.

After chewing up the blackberries, like a mother bird, the Secretary spits the juice into the Bald Minister's expectant mouth. The Bald Minister receives the womanly blackberry juice with childlike joy. He closes his eyes and swishes the nectar in his mouth before swallowing, all his attention focused on his palate, the unique mix of wild blackberry juice and woman's spit. What's more, a nectar served directly from the source, unpasteurised and unmediated.

What the Bald Minister likes most about this tasting is not only the characteristic acidity of the juice but the variations in flavour, if not from day to day, then certainly from week to week. This is not only due to the quality of the blackberries but also to the chemical composition of the Secretary's saliva.

The experienced Bald Minister is able to discern in that nectar the earthy or fruity hints of menstruation or ovulation.

After drinking the juice, the Bald Minister decides to draft a new law.

The recommendable visit

The Director stops cycling.

He dismounts behind a fence near a building in the Brown Zone.

The Director climbs the staircase athletically, four steps at a time, to the third floor. He rings the bell of apartment 407 once.

The Dwarf Prostitute opens the door. Lipstick smudged. Eyes heavily contoured with eyeliner. The Director wipes his number 48 boots on the mat, leans forward to go through the door, enters.

The Redhead has not spread her legs for the Director for two years and a few months.

Throughout their marriage she has had that power: of opening or closing her legs. Lacking the nous or the courage to cope with his unfulfilled desire, and incapable – due to his missing fingers – of using his own hands to relieve himself, the Director would visit apartment 407.

The Dwarf Prostitute did not disdain the visit or the generous payment in the form of meat pies. But as soon as she had shut the door, she would swear at the Director, complaining about the early hour.

God gave whores the morning to rest, she would moan.

*

The Dwarf Prostitute would take advantage of the Director's mild temper or his feigned patience to lash out at the world and its mother. She thought of the Director as a punching bag that she might hit over and over again without any pushback or retort. As inert as a sack of potatoes.

Words like *bastard giant* or *son of an oversized whore* mixed with the saliva that had curdled overnight in her mouth.

The Director took those pungent morning insults on the chin, shrugging his shoulders, and followed her down the hallway. He did not take them seriously. They were barks, nothing but barks, she would not bite. A prostitute is the least dangerous of all women.

And besides, the Director recognised courage, directness and intelligence in the Dwarf Prostitute. She did what she knew how to do, and she knew what she did. With no envy, no fear, no coyness. With no questions. She lied with her body but used no words. That revealed her dignity. Bodies need to exchange fluids, not words. So, between them, the game was fair, the rules were clear. Where there were no affections there could be no lies, and that was as it should be.

Furthermore, these encounters offered the Director moments of great mirth. They were among those few moments where his harelip might pull back to reveal a toothy smile.

He was very large. She was very small. The top of the prostitute's head reached somewhere around the height of his crotch. True, in matters of pleasure and fornication, size and weight do not matter much, but there was still something comic about that inequality of height. The giant, unable to pleasure himself, sought pleasure from a Dwarf Prostitute. And the Dwarf Prostitute complied, reversing their roles: when it came to offering pleasure, the Dwarf Prostitute was the real giant.

Today, along with the dozen meat pies, the Director had given her an orange goldfish swimming in a transparent plastic bag.

The Dwarf Prostitute, holding up the bag, appeared intrigued by the offering. She had never had a pet. She had enough animals to deal with as it was. But a goldfish, that slow goldfish with its curved spine, seemed so blameless. Its indolent gaze gave a sense of innocent indifference.

Yes, she thought, thanking him for the gift: she would adopt it as a silent confidante, a companion that would never judge her.

Testy mattress

After listening to the Dwarf Prostitute's repetitive complaints, the Director advised:

Don't change your bed. This is a good bed. It's a talking bed. It will help you with your business.

As soon as the Director lay down, the springs creaked: the squeals of a hurt animal. The springs protested about the continuous labour into which they were forced. The Dwarf Prostitute's bed was not made only for rest. It was made for working, for moaning, and for making money by moaning. With only her weight on the bed, the mattress had no reason to complain. But with the men's weight added to hers, on top of which there was the force of the pelvic thrusts, then the springs screeched like the Dwarf Prostitute. The screeching of metallic springs and vocal cords, a concert of genuine screeches and fake screeches, to make the men happy, to make them feel powerful, so they could return home fully satisfied, hands in their pockets, whistling, relaxed and light-footed, and ready to return another day, ready to pay more, ready to hear more screeching. What they most wanted was to hear the screaming and moaning: yes, we made a woman squeal like an animal, they told themselves proudly. And that is why they always returned to the talking mattress, to the moaning prostitute. Because at home, fucking was not only rare, but silent.

The Director was enjoying the moment: finally, a bed. Even if it was not big enough for him.

The Director lay lengthwise on the bed, his knees dangling over the edge. He planted his boots on the floor. The Dwarf Prostitute, determined, climbed over the Director's corduroyed knees. She unzipped his trousers. She curved her back like horses do to eat their fodder.

As soon as her mouth started its work, slowly and tenderly, the Director forgot about the flying swans on the lilac-coloured wallpaper and shut his eyes to think about the Redhead: the thin and cold mouth he had kissed before breakfast.

The Director paid the Dwarf Prostitute to be able to lay on her bed and close his eyes, and imagine he was loved by the one who had not spread her legs for him for two years and a few months.

The executioners talk (III): I did something, I have a secret

Neck Brace, the executioner, gazing at the fish tank, sitting on the lurid chair:

What the hell did he do to the fish? There's only one left. I remember six of them. I'm sure. And now just one. It must feel lonely, the poor thing.

He dipped a piece of cake into his coffee mug, put it in his mouth, chewed.

The door opens.

Glass Eye comes in. Remains standing by the door.

He pulls a cigarette out of its pack. Does not light it.

Neck Brace, noting his colleague's presence, says without turning to him:

Did you see the sun? Finally! The bastard showed up! I'm always afraid that he'll decide not to come. Winter is so long. But then, on the right day, there he is. Like a weapon. Never misses.

Glass Eye walks around the desk and sits on the purple velvet chair. An unlit cigarette between his fingers.

So? Not talking much?

No.

When the sun comes out, people are different. Happier.

Sure . . . Where's the giant?

Not here yet. Coffee?

I had one already.

Muffin? It's fresh out of the oven.

Chocolate?

Let's see . . . Not sure what flavours they are. I know they're all sweet. I have . . .

Leave it . . . Listen . . . I need to talk to you before the giant shows up.

Sure.

But eat your muffin first.

So, what's up?

Finish chewing it. I can't talk to you if you're ruminating like that.

What's wrong with it?

Chew properly.

Neck Brace took his time gnashing his jaws, then opened his empty mouth and stuck his tongue out:

Done.

Listen. I've got to tell you something.

Tell me.

It's important.

Go on.

I did something.

You did something?

Yes.

Something you shouldn't have done?

That's right.

Is it a secret?

Yes. Are you paying attention? This is important! Look at me, not the fish tank.

I'm looking at you. Let me just rearrange the chair. Because of my neck. Right, what is it?

It's a secret.

So what? You did something. It's a secret. Is that all?

Yes.

For fuck's sake, we've all done it! This doesn't sound like you at all. C'mon. We've all done shit. Some of it is big, some of it is small. But in the end, it's all the same.

Yes. But my shit was really big. So, it's a big secret. The guilt, the shit, keeping it secret, it all takes up a lot of space, do you get me?

Not really.

It's all shit, that's it.

I got that.

What I did, I did alone. But the secret isn't just mine.

So, whose is it?

Mine and many others'.

So not really a secret, then, if others know.

You don't get it. I knew you wouldn't get it.

Explain yourself, then!

Forget it.

Aren't you going to smoke that cigarette?

Glass Eye throws the cigarette and the lighter across the desk. Neck Brace, with butter fingers, fails to catch either. He leans forward to pick them up . . .

Forget about the bloody cigarette. Listen. This is important!

Yes, dammit, I'm listening. You're in a foul mood!

Glass Eye looks towards the door, then lowers his voice.

Here's the thing: there's a network.

A network.

A network . . . a bit like . . . It's too long to explain.

What kind of network?

People don't always say what they really think.

Yes, but what kind of network?

You wouldn't understand.

What are you trying to say? Just spit it out. I won't understand a thing you're saying if you're saying it like that! You're making me nervous! We've worked together for almost sixteen years. You're like a brother to me.

I know. So are you.

Good.

Glass Eye takes a deep breath, his heart heavy.

What I'm trying to say is that people spend most of their time saying and doing things that are the opposite of what they think. Don't believe anything they say. No matter what.

What?

You have to escape.

Escape?

Yes.

Are you OK?

I am.

You're not well, dammit!

I'm fine! I told you I'm fine! Fuck you!

Glass Eye bangs on the desk to make his point.

Sure. Whatever.

The executioners talk (IV): Do you have black shoes?

Neck Brace, the executioner, eyes fixed on the fish tank, follows the goldfish's presumptuous swimming. And, without knowing quite how, a mental image emerges, clearly. And a great peace comes over him. He has a sort of epiphany. A moment of terrifying clarity. In that instant, Neck Brace understands everything about all things. Everything that had escaped his understanding until then is now revealed: so, in the end, God doesn't see everything. God sees nothing. He had never arrived. He had never been there. Nor did he take sides. And his colleague was now caught in some kind of network. And the fish was caught in the fish tank. And he himself was stuck in a neck brace. And if, nevertheless, God was going to arrive, he was already late. Because he himself, that fish and his colleague were all the same thing. And as ever, all were guilty.

He understood that one is the continuation of the other. And the other the continuation of yet another. And when one is another, the other is the one. In democracy, as in theology: everyone is guilty.

Content in his lucidity, he moves slowly, his back straight. He picks up the cigarette, the lighter. He lights up. Smoke escaping through his nose. Suddenly he says:

I know what you did.
You do?

You talked to the warty guy? You talked to that fucker, didn't you?

Well . . .

And he turned you like he turned the giant. The guy was even allowed visitors.

I didn't speak to the Messenger. I mean . . . I spoke to *Him*.

Him, who?

Names don't matter. I can't . . .

Glass Eye feels his lungs heaving. He bends over on the chair. He falls to the floor on his knees. Puts his hand on his chest. The convulsion seems endless. Shut fist in his mouth. Coughing wildly. He pulls out a handkerchief. Spits on the fabric. Gasps. Examines it. Just what he expected: red.

Neck Brace helps his colleague stand up. Helps him into the purple velvet chair.

You're in a state, you are . . .

Want to see?

Blood!

Yes.

Didn't you go to the doctor?

I have the results here.

And?

Do you have black shoes?

What are you talking about?

Do you have a pair of black shoes?

I have some brown ones, a bit old. But black, plain black, just the boots. Why are you asking?

Buy some black shoes. And a suit.

Why?

Because you'll need them soon. You'll have to visit the Bank.

What? No!

Yes.

But . . . what . . . ?

Listen, you shithead: I have a tumour. It's spread all over.

Neck Brace looks incredulous, opens and closes his mouth three times before saying:

Fuck off!

Yes, you might as well say that. I have a month before I fuck off.

One month!

Look at this.

Glass Eye shows him the bloody handkerchief again.

It's spreading quick.

One month. So, but . . .

Listen: you know that you are like a brother to me.

I know. You are too.

That's why I need to ask you . . .

Ask. Whatever you want. Just ask.

I'm so scared I can't even cry, said Glass Eye, and put his hand over his chest to recover his breath.

Neck Brace had turned pale. He did not say a word. Did not move.

Noting the heavy pause, Glass Eye continued:

No . . . You, you're here. You always were. You're more than a brother. I wouldn't feel so close to a blood brother. The things we've done together.

I know.

Another thing . . .

I'm listening.

No questions. Just do as I say. It might seem strange.

Just say.

I have an envelope.

Yes.

You know that soldier that guards the border of the Yellow Zone?

What soldier?

That soldier in the Yellow Zone.

Which one?

That soldier.

Which one?

You know, dammit!

In the Yellow Zone?

Yes.

What soldier? There are so many.

The one in the Yellow Zone. The strange one. The one with blue eyes.

Oh, that one . . . blue eyes! You could have said. I know him. So what?

Give him this envelope.

Glass Eye puts his hand in his jacket's inner pocket. He puts a sealed envelope into his colleague's hand.

There's no sender.

No.

Who do I say it's from? You?

No, not me, no. Wait. Let me catch my breath.

Glass Eye breathes noisily. He swallows.

I'll give him the envelope and do what?

Nothing.

And what do I say?

Don't say anything.

Nothing?

No.

What's in the envelope?

I don't know.

What the hell? Why don't you deliver it yourself?

Fuck's sake! Just do this thing for me. It's just a fucking envelope! You're more than a brother to me. I only have one month left.

The visit (I): Lowering expectations of good

Because we always have our backs turned, God hardly ever lets us know what *He* will do to us next. And the best thing, the most sensible thing, at times like those, the first thing to do when we feel a light tap on the shoulder, is to expect something bad. To consider the worst possible scenario. Or, at least, to lower our expectations of something good happening. So that, when we finally turn around, we are not taken by surprise – after the high hopes always comes the punch in the face. Otherwise, God pushes us roughly into a corner and hits us with the power of the eternal. *He* has us crying, enraged, protesting:

After all my prayers, it's not fair!

What have I done to not be among the chosen ones?

The Worker knew this. He knew what to expect and had agreed, opposing no resistance, to the fatal outcome. There was no alternative. If he refused, he could jeopardise everything. And besides, he was not afraid of death. Faith feeds off death. And he knew its smell, its entrails, its anatomy. He believed in a ticket to paradise. One way, no return. But as soon as he arrived in the Factory's main office, and one of the three soldiers told him that he was expected at the Prison in an hour's time, and despite the stalk of his faith being well watered, he could feel a scream getting caught in his throat. Something had happened. He swallowed hard, but the fear remained. It was still there, behind his larynx, waiting for the right opportunity. Something had happened, of course. But what? The Worker considered some possibilities. No, it couldn't be the Messenger. God would not have allowed it. *He* was God's voice on Earth and was stronger than anyone. He innocently asked the soldier with the highest rank why he was being summoned, as if he were going to get an answer. Instead of the answer came an order: show up at the gates of the Factory's south wing in ten minutes' time, without your Factory smock, before moving on.

The Worker complied. And as he walked, taking heavy steps towards the locker room, he could not avoid the nagging doubts. Had the Little Man been wagging his tongue? He had never trusted him. The Dwarf Prostitute? No . . . And what if it had been his sister? He opened the door to the locker room. His heart was weak. And a weak heart is often an unloved heart. Easy to manipulate in moments of fragility. By his locker he took off his bloodied smock. Had the giant discovered the maps and notes about the plan while they were distracted? The Worker felt dizzy as he considered this possibility. As it was mid-shift, the locker room was empty. He leaned against the door to regain his balance. He staggered towards the sinks. He put his hands on the ceramic rim, looked into the mirror, lowered his neck, opened the tap, put his hands under the stream, filled his cupped hands, raised the water to his face, looked into his own eyes, studied the acne-scarred skin shimmering with waterdrops, noticed a ripe pimple, raised his index fingers to his forehead, and as he pressed one firmly against the other, the squeezed fatty pimple exploded onto the mirror.

He shut the tap. Wiped his face on a towel. Licked his finger and touched the bloodied pore. The dizziness had passed. Ready. He was now calm.

The visit (II): The sheep is silent in the hands of those who shear it

The Worker followed Neck Brace into the visitors' room. The Messenger was sitting at a low table. His hands uncuffed, interlaced fingers on the tabletop. Seeing him alive and well, the Worker felt enormous relief. Like menthol on his chest. His heart felt lighter, fresher. His frightened eyes gleamed. And he promised himself that he would not cry, come what may.

Neck Brace pointed towards the empty chair. He shot the Worker a hard look:

I don't know how you managed this, wart face. But God knows it's not a good idea. I know enough about the affairs of men to know that this isn't good. If I were in charge, you'd be . . . You'd have been sent off to a little place I know . . . Anyway . . . You have fifteen minutes.

The Worker sat in the empty chair. Neck Brace glanced at both men one last time and left the room. If he could, he would have shaken his head. Instead, he slammed the door. His way of saying: I don't agree with this.

Soon after the door slammed shut, the Worker looked around. He looked at the Messenger. And then he got up, to embrace him. Tears ran, small, loose, fast, happy. He took in the Messenger's smell. He kissed his shaved head, his forehead. He offered his lips. The Messenger pushed him away delicately.

Be patient. We don't have much time.

Can we talk?

We can.

Sure?

Yes.

Are you certain?

Trust me.

How did you manage it?

Did you doubt I'd be able to?

No, of course not.

You should know: *He* is with me. *He* never leaves me.

I know. I never doubted.

I know you didn't.

The two men remained still for a few seconds.

The Messenger cracked his knuckles.

The Worker looked at his warts and took his hands.

You're so thin. If I'd known I was seeing you, I would have smuggled in some pies.

Don't worry. I'm fine. How about you?

I've been praying. For you. For us.

You look well. Your skin.

I'm using a new cream. It seems to be working.

The Messenger nodded.

How are things at the Factory?

They're . . . I mean . . . Those animals . . . *He* should not allow it . . .

The Messenger pulled the Worker towards him.

Don't forget: He *was oppressed, but didn't open* His *mouth; like a lamb,* He *was driven to slaughter, but like the sheep is silent in the hands of those who shear it,* He *didn't open* His *mouth.* We are so close. It's not worth the risk.

When?

Soon. When the crow caws.

The visit (III): My crow wants to caw

My crow wants to caw.

In response, the Messenger released the Worker.

And for the first time, the Messenger smiled. He raised his hand to his lumpy nose, pressed on his nostrils, snorted. Having deployed the right words, the Worker felt caterpillars crawling in his stomach, and then turning into fluttering butterflies. Suddenly, and in a succession of decisive gestures: he stood up, pushed the chair away, turned around, pulled down his trousers and pants and stuck out his buttocks: two lean moons, one of them tattooed with an open-beaked crow.

See? He wants to caw. For you.

I would very much like to hear him caw. But we have no time. Be patient.

The Worker felt embarrassed for not having kept his impulse in check. His eyes were filled with shame. Maybe he was being selfish and disobedient. Wanting too much, when he should have been contented with little. And if there were time, that little would be everything. But when a heart is hungry, a single crumb will never be enough.

He tried to recover his composure as best he could. Recover his dignity.

He sat down and crossed his arms.

What happened to your teeth?

The Messenger smiled indulgently. He cracked his knuckles.

Cavities. I had terrible pain. They had to pull them out and they gave me these new ones.

But those aren't your own! It was them, wasn't it? Those bastards!

The Worker shakes his head. Fat tears, slow, dense, unhappy.

Shhh, whispered the Messenger, kindly. Save them for the day. Not long to go. I have everything under control. All will be well, you'll see.

You always say that . . .

Because it's true.

Yes, but the day never comes . . .

I promise you: when you least expect it, it will happen.

I've done nothing else but wait, wait, wait . . . *He* shouldn't allow it.

You have to be patient. Trust me.

The Messenger raised his gaze towards the ceiling and looked at the plaster as if he were staring at a far-away sky.

It's difficult to know what *His* thoughts are. They're too high up for us.

I know, I know. You're right. I'm sorry. I'm being selfish.

We all are. But just turn the other cheek. Not long to go. We once had nothing, remember?

I remember.

Onwards, then: did you distribute the manna?

Yes. We're ready. We just await your crow.

And did your sister say anything?

About the giant?

And about the Redhead.

A letter arrived yesterday. She writes every week. In her latest she wrote that she came across the giant in the laundry room, bent over the laundry basket and fishing out some knickers.

Your sister's?

My sister's and the Redhead's.

To examine and sniff them.
How do you know?
The Messenger looked at him, smirking.
The Worker laughed.
Sorry, it was a stupid question.
And the treasure?
The box?
Yes.
He has it already.
Excellent. All will be well, you'll see.
I know. I believe you. I never doubted.
Listen.
The Messenger takes his hands.
What?
Don't talk. Just listen.
The Worker half shut his eyes and opened his ears to the silence.
After listening for some time, he asked: What is it?
Can't you hear it?
No.
Music.

The sun moves across the sky, and everyone wants to be (II)

With the arrival of summer, in the Forest, insects awaken from their blank sleep to flap wings and rehearse flights. In newly formed puddles they prepare their weapons. They refine their segmented bodies. They free themselves of the humid soil, chirping with their abdomens. And, from within their exoskeletons, they release the pheromones that trigger rituals of procreation.

In the Forest, insects outnumber humans and stars put together.

But they are not satisfied: they want to be more.

Gymnopédie IX

The Formula: A brief summary of the Bald Minister's most important sayings

The formula for the natural attraction between x and y, between male and female – with a few obvious exceptions, which always exist – is this:

x expects some response from whoever she has chosen: ranging from y^1 to y^{354}

When x is prepared to get a response, she signals to her chosen one: $x^2 = x + \ldots$

After the signalling, it is a matter of observing the speed and thoroughness of reaction of the chosen one (chosen sometimes by sheer dint of proximity). An example:

$$x^2 = x + y^{12}$$

And so this y^{12} is the lucky one. Or the unlucky one. It all depends.

In a room where the bed is never wrong

The heat lifts the dust.

The singing of crickets and cicadas breaks through the air in two distinct notes. The crickets and cicadas are singing about the snow that imprisoned them. And the sun that has now freed them. The singing of crickets and cicadas travels over the Wall. It runs through the streets. It enters all homes. Even the ones with closed windows.

On a street that runs parallel to 22nd Street, the horse's elegant legs stop.

The Lame Soldier slides off the saddle. He ties the reins to a gate. He hears the uneven sound of his boots on the gravel.

Behind him, the horse neighs.

As he walks away, the Lame Soldier says:

In the summer, unlike the winter, it's not a man's footprints that betray him, but the sound of his steps.

After climbing the fifty-seven steps, breathing hard and with sweat gathering in the curls on his forehead, the Lame Soldier rings the bell of apartment 407 twice. He looks to both sides of the empty hallway. Neglected doormats outside the numbered doors welcome the hot and slow dust as it settles.

On the tips of her toes, standing on a wooden stool, the Dwarf Prostitute looks through the door's peephole. She is indisposed. Her morning mood is as sour as lime juice on an empty stomach.

She is exhausted. She had worked all night at the Club and deserves some rest. Her mouth still tastes of last night's semen. She has no reason to complain: that is her job. But she is worn out, depleted, sore. In need of beauty sleep and repair. Still, despite the tiredness accumulated in her flesh, the Dwarf Prostitute knows that when it came to this Lame Soldier, her job had greater purpose and reach. There was a sense of mission. She heard the internal whisper of the Messenger's sacred words:

You will be my army of untouched hearts and innocent hands. Turn your enemies into a cobbled path for your feet. Pile up their corpses and smash the impious heads. Give the arrogant the punishment they deserve.

These words made her unlatch the door, step off the stool, push it away with one foot, and turn the doorknob with her long fingernails painted green.

The Lame Soldier smiles. Takes off his beret. Wipes the sweat off his brow. Steps into apartment 407 with his good leg first. The Lame Soldier believes that stepping into a home with his good leg first brings good luck.

The Dwarf Prostitute, her dressing gown crumpled, hair in disarray, makeup smudged, looks up and sees the shaven head. The gun's leather strap slung over the shoulder. The Lame Soldier smiles again. He has picked up the Dwarf Prostitute's briny smell: the perfume covering the odour of sweat to aid seduction.

In the bedroom, the brown velvet curtains are blocking the light from the outside. This change of atmosphere, added to the stagnant smells of overnight fornication, make the Lame Soldier dizzy. He sits down on the bed.

The bed moans.

*

In a bedroom the bed is never wrong. In a bedroom a prostitute is never wrong. Sitting on a prostitute's bed, a man simply adds, and is added up. He ceases to be a soldier, a doctor, a minister, a worker. He loses all status and power. In a prostitute's bed, a man simply is: a *one* added to other *ones* in a daily tally.

In a bedroom with swans and a goldfish

Despite being armed, the Lame Soldier feels powerless. A light fatigue takes over. Women engage in the most dangerous combat. He asks for a drink. Alcohol always helps to regain courage.

The Dwarf Prostitute lets her dressing gown slip open and walks towards the kitchen. The Lame Soldier follows the movement of the light fabric as it draws the contour of her plump and disproportionate shape. The compact flesh, prevented from expanding by shortened bones.

He throws his beret onto the wardrobe. The beret lands near a small mirror, knocking over some pieces of the already untidy arsenal of cosmetics.

The Lame Soldier scratches his shaved head and looks at the wallpaper. Over a lilac-coloured background, a flock of white swans are taking flight towards the stuccoed ceiling. He picks up his gun. Shuts one eye. He frames a swan in the gun's sight. Then another. Pretends to shoot, imitating the sounds of gunshot. Then he notices the round fishbowl on the nightstand, inside which a goldfish, slow and with a curved spine, swims around with a withered fin.

He points at the fish.

The Dwarf Prostitute returns with a glass in her hand.

He puts down his gun. And drinks, without taking his eyes off the fishbowl.

His tongue sweeps across his moustache. He asks:

Where did the fish come from?

A gift.

It's odd.

It has a crooked spine.

That's not it. I feel like I know it.

The fish? It's a bit like you, except it swims crooked instead of walking crooked.

That's not it. I've seen it before. Can't remember where.

Really?

Yes, I'm sure. I just can't remember where.

The Lame Soldier makes an effort: he tugs at the elastic strings of memory.

Don't be silly, all fish are the same, says the Dwarf Prostitute, to bring the matter to a close. She takes off her dressing gown. She unveils the spectacle of silk, garters, lace. A festival of flesh.

A pair of small and pointy breasts lights up the Lame Soldier's face.

Confronted with that vision, the Lame Soldier stops worrying about the fish, puts his glass down, takes the plunge.

She holds his sweaty shaved head, brings the Lame Soldier's mouth close to her belly button. She whispers:

I hardly recognised you . . .

I grew a moustache . . . And you dyed your hair.

I always do. It's summer. I need to change things. If not, I get bored. Men are not so easily bored. But I get bored with myself.

Did you also dye your hair down there?

She pulls her knickers' elastic back with one of her green fingernails. The Lame Soldier takes a peek.

No, I shaved.

Very good.

The sun brings changes.

In a bed where the whore is a saint:
An exchange of goods

The Dwarf Prostitute moves away, towards the chest of drawers, offering him a vision of her fat buttocks.

Her knowledge and experience about men's weaknesses, partnered to her erudition about the body and the laws of desire, and the valleys and peaks of pleasure, tells her: move away a little, desire needs to be kept waiting and salivating.

She absent-mindedly retouches her lipstick.

Did you bring what I asked for?

Shall we carry on . . . ?

Answer me first.

Cut out the bullshit.

What do you want this time?

You know . . .

No, I don't.

Don't play the innocent.

No, I'm playing the whore.

You never change.

I'm a saint.

A saint and a whore?

Whore and saint. Whore: because I give what you see, to men like you, for a price, so that in this life there are moments when pleasure lasts longer than pain. Saint: because in those moments, you and the others, through me, catch a glimpse of heaven. And while you are here fucking me, you are not out there breaking bottles and giving women and children bruises and black eyes.

You never change. You make me laugh. Saintly whore.

Laughing and coming – the two things you can't lie about.

Whatever, come on, carry on where you left . . .

Did you bring what I asked for?

I'll give them to you after.

No, first you pay, then you get.

What do you need them for?

The tablets? To sleep for four days in a row when it's that time of month.

What time of month?

When I'm on my period.

Oh. But no, I meant: what do you need the passes for?

So that some of my colleagues can breathe new air, see new colours, meet new cocks. In this Zone, when the wind is blowing, the smell from the Factory becomes unbearable. And as we can't just jump over the Wall . . .

Whatever. I give up.

Good idea.

With a resigned smile, the Lame Soldier pulls out of his pocket the six passes with the stamp allowing free access to all Zones in the City, and a box of tablets.

Here they are. As requested. Now . . . Can you please continue?

The Dwarf Prostitute moves back towards the bed. Desire has salivated enough.

You deserve a bit of suck-suck. Or what else do you want this time?

Some things are worth repeating. You're good at repeating.

So, you want me to serve you the Bald Minister's favourite dish? You want me to dance?

Stop, enough teasing . . . Do you want me to put a bullet in you?

Relax, big boy, no need to grow impatient. Let's calm that beast down. Let me show you heaven in my bedroom.

Kilometres in the dreamworld: A seagull in the Forest

Despite the thick mattress in his new cell, the two hundred crunches and the one hundred push-ups, the fourteen laps of the Prison's yard, the Messenger had had a restless night. He had woken up soaked in sweat. Breathless. His muscles aching. Exhausted from dreaming. There are dreams that demand a more intense physical effort than that required for some athletic activities. Indeed, that morning, as he opened his eyes, the Messenger felt as if he had been unknowingly running through the night, completing a course of forty-two kilometres plus a few extra metres in the dreamworld.

The Director burst in, clean-shaven. With a smile that stretched his harelip's now visible scar. And without being invited, he immediately sat on the camp bed, besides the self-absorbed Messenger, as if they were old cellmates.

Probing the mattress's thickness with his right glove, he said:

Lucky you: not even I have such a good bed!

The Messenger did not respond. Nor did he seem surprised by the Director's visit. As with so many other things happening, he had foreseen this one too. But there was something in the Director's tone, even in the way he moved, that was unexpected. The Messenger knew how important this visit was. How much effort he needed to put into it. But the night had left deep marks. Lazily, almost indifferent, with his right index finger massaging his new front teeth, he let the Director talk while he tried to piece together the images he had seen in his dreams.

The Director spoke non-stop for fifteen minutes. The Messenger picked out what was most important in the monologue: map, X, snow, wolves, box, fingers, icebox. Nothing new. Everything had happened as planned. Perhaps that was why the Messenger had used those fifteen minutes to examine his recent dreams. Why had *He* sent a seagull to meet him in the middle of the Forest? Not an angel, not the wolves, not a bear, not the long-expected crow, not an annoying dove, not a whale, but a seagull. And this seagull had squawked from high up in a fir tree and then launched itself onto him. Attacked him. What did this mean? How should he interpret this divine message? This seagull attack, in the middle of the Forest?

The Director finished and patted his knees with his gloves, getting up to leave.

So that's what happened, he said.

The Messenger pulled his finger out of his mouth and rubbed his spit on one of the warts on his left hand. He looked at the ceiling.

I suppose you have another question for me, Director?

Yes. You know what it is.

I do.

So?

The answer to the question you want to ask is: go ask the Blond Doctor.

The Blond Doctor?

Yes, the Blond Doctor. Go ask him.

Medical examination (I): Including a stupid question and scratching of earlobe

After the rectal examination, the Nurse releases the Blond Doctor's manicured hands from the tight latex gloves. The Director has his trousers and pants around his ankles. Hairy buttocks wide open.

The Blond Doctor flattens his uncombed eyebrow, using his examining figure and a bit of spit. The Nurse throws the latex gloves into a bin lined with a green plastic bag. She exits to wash her hands. The door closes silently.

The Director gets off the examination table and looks at the Blond Doctor. He pulls up his pants and trousers to cover himself. Despite knowing well enough what brought him there, he cannot hide the embarrassment and humiliation he was just subjected to. And, as if that were not enough, he now had to ask the stupid question. The fateful question. The fundamentally foolish question. The humiliating question that does not deserve to be asked: it was his body, after all, and he was always living in it. And no one should know how to repair it better than the person that carries it around. So unfair! So worthy of revolt! But after enough time to pull up his zipper with his gloved index and middle fingers, the words come straight out of the Director's throat:

Is it serious?
We'll need to run a few more tests.

But is it a kidney stone?

The Director sits down in the patient's chair.

The Doctor, sitting in the green velvet chair, replies:

It's the prostate. It may be benign hyperplasia.

Prostate? You sure?

I didn't give you a rectal examination just for fun, Director.

Really?

It's enlarged. It's grown with age.

The Director assesses the Doctor's hands.

I don't care what it is. Will I be able to piss like I should?

Don't worry. If it's benign, as I think it is, with the right medication you'll be urinating normally.

Good.

The Blond Doctor spreads his manicured fingers and combs back his hair. He looks at the Director and feels the moment is right to play his winning card. The idea had been on his mind from the moment the appointment was confirmed.

He leans forward and opens a drawer.

I have the test results, Director.

What test results? I haven't had any new tests yet.

The Blond Doctor shows him a yellow envelope with the Hospital's stamp.

Test results for your wife, Director.

What tests?

Routine tests. Mammography. Pap smear.

Pap smear? What's the problem?

It's confidential.

What's wrong with her?

It's confidential.

The Messenger was right, the Director thinks: that whore and this sonofabitch.

Tell her to come see me tomorrow with the greatest urgency.

So you can feel her up again?

No, so your wife can open the envelope. To talk about her test results.

It's so easy to be a doctor.

Excuse me?

It's so easy . . . You take advantage of having the access code to the body.

What access code?

You know.

Do I?

Don't play the fool. Consider my case: I have great power, but then I come here, and I have to pull my trousers and pants down.

The Blond Doctor rehearses a sinister smile.

You forget one thing, Director.

What's that?

It's not an access code.

What is it?

It's the doctor's coat that separates us.

What do you mean?

You don't wear a doctor's coat, Director. I, on the other hand, use a white doctor's coat. I took an oath. When I wear that white coat, I'm not an ordinary man.

You scratched your earlobe, Doctor.

So?

You scratched your earlobe. You're lying.

Don't be silly!

You scratched your earlobe. It's so easy to spot your tell. Your right hand betrayed you. It would be easier for you if you were a woman. Women are better liars when they have to be. Women always know more than they let on, and they always hide part of what they know.

Thrush: A flower about to blossom

The Redhead shakes her sad curls:

It had to happen just now. Only five days before the big recital.

The Redhead believes that her curls had lost some of their happiness, their bounce, their volume, since that night spent in the stables with the Lame Soldier.

The silk robe slides over the skin.

It lands elegantly at the foot of the bed.

The towel is stretched over the bedspread. The Redhead raises her knee. She sits on her haunches with the glass jar to hand. The mattress springs complain about an unusual position that they are unaccustomed to. There is creaking and squeaking, and the grinding of joints and kneecaps, until the Redhead finds a stable balance.

Before starting the procedure, the Redhead takes a few sips of tea. She swallows two brown tablets. She glances at the locked door. She feels an itch, a burning sensation. She cannot risk anyone walking in. Finding her in that position.

The Redhead puts a small scoop of natural yoghurt into her vagina. She is not using gloves. She had sanitised her hands earlier. And she had filed her fingernails to avoid hurting herself. She feels the brief relief of the cold yoghurt coming into contact with her feverish flesh. She puts two fingers into the jar.

Takes a larger scoop. The burning is constant. The itch, unbearable. As if down there, in her nether region, tireless ants were hard at work. Hundreds of little black legs, dancing non-stop.

She needs to drown them. Smother them in fermented milk. The *acidophilus* will kill them, sooner or later.

The Redhead fills her primordial orifice with the white substance. Trembling, refreshing. Once, and then again.

Legs bent, the Redhead stoppers her vagina with a delicate hand. She uses her fingers as a plug to prevent the cure from leaking out. She moves out of the uncomfortable squat and stretches on the bed.

The Redhead pulls the pillow towards her. She buries her head in it. She concentrates on the singing of crickets and cicadas. She must keep the yoghurt inside her for as long as possible, the Blond Doctor had said. So that the good bacteria can do their dutiful combat against evil.

The fingertips tap at her orifice's entrance.

This process of filling herself with yoghurt is arousing.

And the Redhead's thoughts once again sneak off towards the stables. Towards the night when the Lame Soldier knew her. And when she allowed herself to be known. And when by knowing that lame man, with an exuberant smell and an exuberant penis, her vaginal flora was altered.

Thrush is the new name.

Acquired after the night spent at the stables.

Thrush is the name of a flower.

And the Redhead feels that flower blossoming inside her.

Medical examination (II): When others open their hearts, and another access code

The Blond Doctor took a moment to digest those words. And to try to understand what the Director was getting at, to avoid any missteps and trip-ups in the dark. He finally said:

If that's really how you feel, Director, why are you here? If you doubt my skills . . .

On the contrary, I fully trust your technical knowledge. Your instincts, however . . . are another matter.

What do you mean?

Let me explain. Instincts are the foundations for this edifice we call Man. They are the foundations on which the pillars of our aptitudes and capacities and intelligence will be built. If those instincts are shaky, if they suffer from subsidence, then no matter how robust the pillars are, the whole edifice will be at risk of sliding and collapsing. The edifice – in other words, Man – will be crooked. Do you see?

The Blond Doctor does not respond. He is buying time.

I'll say it again: I don't have the access code to the body. Only to the soul. And, as you know, the body always triumphs over the soul. If we relied only on our souls, we'd be immortal . . .

Some people do believe that.

I'm not one of them.

I can see you're upset, and I regret that your wife . . .

Don't be a hypocrite! I know what's going on!

Do you?

Yes.

And what is going on?

The Director is losing his patience:

Listen. Don't make me waste my words. Better to drop the act. We both know what's going on. I'll confess something. In spite of everything, I love my wife. Sixteen years ago, I opened my heart and let her make a choice. And she chose me. It wasn't easy to be chosen, you know? And I don't like others opening their hearts to her.

I'm afraid I'm not following.

So let me clarify things: I propose an agreement.

An agreement?

Yes. I believe you're very familiar with the words with which agreements are sealed. Am I wrong?

The Blond Doctor feels the sting of the barbed comment. He was not expecting that. His face loses its pallor. He hides his hands behind the desk.

The rules are simple. I give you something and you give me something in return.

And what will you give me, asks the Doctor, his voice faltering with fear.

Something important.

What do you mean?

Your life.

Excuse me?

I have the access code to death.

Oh . . . ?

Yes. In two weeks there will be an execution by firing squad in the Prison. The session will be witnessed by the Bald Minister and other illustrious Party members. Anyone that has been accused of subversion, anyone who committed a grave crime or confessed to plotting against the Government will be summarily executed.

I didn't do anything that . . .

Let me ask you a question: did the Small Man say anything?

Who?

Come, now. Cards on the table. I'm showing you my hand.

What do you want me to say?

Better if you ask: what do I want you to do?

Oh . . .

Yes, time to put cards on the table. Show me your hands.

What?

Show me . . . You have such well-cared-for hands, Doctor . . . Such elegant fingers . . .

I can't . . .

Of course you can. You can and you will. As you know well, I was given a map with an X marking the spot where treasure was buried. I went there and dug up the treasure. I'd like you to assess the quality and the provenance of that treasure. And if that treasure doesn't work, we'll have a problem. You, Doctor, will have to find me another one that works. Do you understand?

But . . .

Yes, that's right. Now show me your hands. Let's play.

Will smiles rise or fall?

He opens the tap.

The bath fills up.

The Worker tests the water. Says a prayer.

He plunges the dirty smock and pulls it back out, repeatedly, like an informer being tortured to reveal secrets.

On his knees on the floor, he concentrates his strength on his knuckles. He rubs the crusty blood out of the cotton fabric. After much scrubbing, the stains dissolve. He unplugs the bath. Redcurrant-coloured water is sucked down the drain. He applies bleach to the persistent stains. Fills the tub once again. The smock floats to the surface: a sallow drowned body, already bloated by the sea.

The butcher's skin that the Worker wears daily is now clean, and his sins are redeemed.

But soon, happily, never again.

In the bedroom, the afternoon light comes in through the cracks. It lights up the dresser on which the holy book rests. The Worker raises the blinds. Opens the window. The eight metres of greyness block his view of the horizon. But looking up at the sky, which is still allowed, he contemplates the colour scale unrolling around the setting sun: smears of lilac and tongues of fire-orange move across the blue, announcing the day's demise.

There is movement on the street. Signs of life.

Pale children, holding hands, run with large smiles. A young couple pushes a pram. An old woman, under the shade of an awning, holds a piece of bread with trembling hands. Three young women, wearing skimpy clothes, finally reveal the sensuality sequestered during the dark months. Government employees, wearing blue vests, sweep the streets and pavements. Others, on top of scaffolding, wielding paint brushes and rollers, retouch the facades of weather-damaged buildings. Soldiers sweat into their uniforms, mounted on panting horses. Rusty bicycles chase after one another. People walk past each other and exchange greetings, caught up in a wholesome excitement, shaken by laughter with no memory. As if they had not been alive yesterday. And would not be alive tomorrow.

The Worker looks at that fleeting happiness with disgust.

He says:

Those smiles will disappear. It hasn't happened yet, true, but it will. Soon the crow will caw.

He closes the window. Lowers the blinds.

Gymnopédie X

The Death: A brief summary of the Bald Minister's most important sayings

Death occupies – unnecessarily, let us say it – a vast physical space. And it is senseless, to avoid using a worse word, to waste so many square metres of surface on crosses, graves and stone angels, coffins, bones and empty crania, not to mention the maggots.

To kill flowers only to comfort the dead, to console those who can no longer produce anything, is also an act of pure evil and wastefulness.

A law based on the obligation to cremate after death allows us to reclaim many metres of our urban space. A small box of 20 x 20 centimetres should suffice to keep the charred remains and preserve the memory. And even with deaths continuing to happen, the City's space does not need to be extended beyond the Wall. All we need to do is dig into the earth, like moles. And to design, in an underground field, an Ash Bank, where widows and widowers, orphans and all who have been tapped on the shoulder by death, can find the ones they loved and the ones they hurt in small, numbered niches. And each will have a key corresponding to their box and their dead. To speak to them in a unique and well-organised space.

A spider, eight legs and the Cat

The Maid takes off a shoe. She slams it down three times, then another. On that fourth attempt, the thick heel hits the spider as it tries to scurry away over the tiles.

The spider leaps, gazelle-like. One of its eight legs has been severed by the heel. The spider makes a squeaking noise. It lets out a silky squeal. Mousse-yellow.

Of the seven legs still attached to its abdomen, six are still. The seventh is still moving, autonomous and arrogant, as if trying to escape, oblivious to death. Whereas the other six were already well aware of it.

Fifteen centimetres away, the eighth leg, the one severed from the body by the blow of the heel, is also wriggling. The two legs convulsed in synchrony. One, still attached. The other, already free. There is still energy there. This dance lasts for fifteen seconds.

Watching the spasms of the eighth leg, the one detached from the body, the Maid remembers a scene from her childhood. She sees the butcher's knife in her mother's hand falling onto the chicken's neck on the wooden stump. She sees the head fly off like a cork. She sees her mother put the decapitated chicken on the floor, for a final lap around the gravelled garden.

It must be sad to die separated from the body in which you always lived, the Maid thinks. And, with a note of disgust, she picks up the eighth leg and puts it next to the squashed body.

She exits the kitchen to find a broom and a dustpan.

The Cat, vigilant, jumps off the refrigerator. He approaches, one paw in front of the other, licking his whiskers. And, with dilated pupils, he swallows and chews the whole spider.

Before knocking on the door: The heart mocks reason

It had been a while since they had exchanged the minimum number of words required for the exchange to be called a conversation, and that bothered him. A wall of minutes that became hours, and hours that had become years, had grown between them, covered in the ivy of silence and rancour. And those few meagre words exchanged between them as the silent barrier grew had been no more than orphaned birds stopping, briefly, to rest their wings, sharpen their beaks, drink drops of dew, and then take off again in search of the flock they had lost.

It was true, the Director and the Redhead had forgotten how to communicate. And every day added to a past filled with silences made it more difficult to restart, to grow the muscles and the will to jump over the barrier.

The Director would have wanted to have a speech ready, but all his efforts were fruitless. He knew what he wanted, or he thought he knew, but he could not get his ideas in order. The phrases that came into his mind were fighting between themselves, savagely, with spears and knives, to come out on top. They engaged in fierce combat. First, I should say this. No, no, you can only say it after saying that. So, I'll say that, and only then I'll say this . . .

It was clear: the Director was rusty when it came to using the language of marriage. His husbandly words. But he was not going to give up. Absolutely not. Especially not now. He was going to confront the Redhead as he had not done before. And he was going to tell her certain things . . . He just did not know which ones.

The heart often mocks reason.

After knocking at the door, one enters: The singing of crickets and cicadas

The Director knocked on the door using his gloved left index finger. It was a soft knock. Almost a whisper. Even so, the Redhead heard it. She stood up from her bed. Turned the latch twice, turned the doorknob. She stretched her swan-like neck. She looked at him, her freckles shining like stars. The green iris growing.

The Director lowered his eyes, scratched his face.

We need to talk.

Finally.

What?

You shaved your beard.

The Director insisted.

We need to talk. May I come in?

The Redhead did not reply. She turned her unruly curls to him and walked, determined, towards the bed. The curls were so thick that they resembled bird nests. The bedroom window was half-open. Summer light, entwined with the voices of crickets and cicadas, entered through the blinds, seeped through the moons in the curtain, and remained there, in silence.

I don't want any shouting, she said, sitting on the bed.

She tightened her dressing gown across her chest. Crossed her legs. She was closing up.

The crickets and cicadas were not between those walls, they

were far away. But they seemed to be right there, beneath the bed. Singing beneath their feet.

The Director bowed his head and crossed the threshold.

He shut the door behind him.

He remained standing, still, calm. Connected to an inner peace. The calming tablets he had taken before coming were the tranquil ground that attached the Director to life. And even if the Redhead invited him to sit down, he would refuse and remain standing. He wanted to see her from above and wanted her to see him as he was: a very tall man. He took his time. He knew that the longer the silence stretched, the more unnerved she would be. And that might be a good thing. Nervous people, when they open their mouths, often say more than they would want to.

The long-postponed conversation (I)

The Director noticed the calf of the Redhead's crossed leg, uncovered by the silk dressing gown. Strong, pale, luminous, beautifully curved.

Still a beautiful woman, with curves to die for, and I still love her, he thought.

The Redhead noticed him noticing and covered herself. She was not going to allow him a glimpse of that landscape.

The Director had not been in that bedroom for a long time. Everything seemed to be arranged as he remembered it, and in the same place. But the smell. That smell coming off the Redhead and clinging to his nostrils was new. A true banquet for his nose. The Director imagined sinking his nose into the Redhead's armpits and becoming inebriated with that ravishing essence. He wanted to live inside her armpits. But his flight of olfactory fancy was abruptly interrupted.

Do you still know how to do it?

How to shave?

How to talk. How long since you came through that door? Do you know?

No.

Nor do I.

Two years?

Don't know. Lost count.

We need to talk.

You said that already.

Do you want to talk?

You're the one who came knocking.

I see what you're trying to do. So this is it: I need to talk to you. Do you want to talk to me?

I don't know.

So, why did you let me in?

I don't know.

Who knows, then?

Letting you in means nothing. Nothing, you hear me? If you want to talk, just talk.

Silence. But he was not going to give up. He would not run away like other times. Not now.

I thought you didn't like yoghurt, the Director said when he saw the empty pot on the nightstand.

I didn't.

And now you do?

There are many things about me that you don't know.

Perhaps.

Perhaps, what?

Perhaps.

So, say what you're here to say so we're done with it.

Is that what you want?

To be done?

Yes.

Perhaps.

In the Redhead's voice, that *perhaps* sounded drier and harder than the word's uncertainty might suggest. She uncrossed and crossed her legs, now showing her other calf. She was itchy and filled with yoghurt. Uncrossing and crossing her legs helped relieve the discomfort, if only for a few brief seconds.

*

The Director interpreted her gesture as an effort in seduction. His eyes fixed on hers and, freed of the bladder discomfort and the trembling eyelid, more confident than ever, he said:

Don't even try. I know you spread your legs for someone else.
You know?
Yes.
You must be happy.
Happy?
You got what you wanted.
What was that?
You pushed me into being with someone else.
Don't make me laugh.
It makes me sad.
What?
That I can, and you can't.
Be with someone else?
No, make you laugh. You don't make me laugh any more.
But perhaps I can still make you cry.
I don't know.
So this isn't over yet. There might still be some tears.
Don't count on it. Tears don't serve any purpose.

The Director was waiting for them – a meaningful number of theatrical tears of regret – but they did not come. He scratched his well-trimmed sideburn. He heard the crickets, the cicadas . . .

I wish I'd heard it from you.
The Redhead, drily, her green eye filled with spite:
Would it have excited you more?
Excited me more?
If I had told you. In full detail.
Maybe.
I thought so.
I'm not interested now.
Let's carry on, then.

The Director paused for a moment. He knew that the conversation was on the brink of skidding down that steep and muddy hill that was so well known to so many. The Redhead's rage was obstinate, it did not recede. He sought out in vain the pair of disparately coloured eyes. He took a deep breath. He would need to try a different approach.

Why do you hate me?

That's such a childish question. You're like a child.

We are all children, always. Until the end.

So, what's the point of growing up?

Why do you hate me?

You let me escape. You didn't hold me.

The long-postponed conversation (II): I can't hear the crickets or the cicadas

The Director says:

Come on, you're not being reasonable.

What does it mean to be reasonable?

You know.

No, I don't know.

Right . . . There's one thing I want to say.

Finally.

Finally, what?

Finally, you're saying whatever's on your mind.

The Redhead raised a fingernail painted in yellow and pointed at the suede gloves.

You're wrong about that.

Am I?

I don't trust you. I don't trust myself. I don't trust anyone apart from our Son.

You bastard! What's our Son got to do with anything? If this is what you've come to talk about, you can forget it! After all this time! Get the hell out!

You said you didn't want any shouting. You're shouting. I can't hear the crickets and the cicadas with your shouting.

Go to hell! Bastard!

The Redhead put her pale hands over her incredulous eyes, on her unruly curls, her thin lips, her trembling knees.

Calm down.

I'll calm down whenever I want.

We've had this conversation before.

That's what marriage is, you bastard! Repetition.

You don't understand. You'll never understand.

It's you that'll never understand!

People need to keep some secrets.

So they'll be heavier when they die?

It isn't that, goddammit.

The Director looked at her. He was sweating. A vein was throbbing on his temple.

It isn't that . . . If I had told you what happened that night, it wouldn't have changed anything. I'd already lost them . . . If I had told you how everything happened, in full detail, blow by blow, I'm sure I would have lost control. If I had told you how everything happened, there would have been no mystery. And it would have changed nothing, the damage was done. I made a mistake. And I had to pay for it. Me, you understand? I wanted to spare you.

Spare me? I can't believe it! Spare me? So clever . . . You spared me, and by doing so you lost me.

Are you serious?

I am.

I don't get it.

Neither do I.

Who are you?

And you, who the hell are you?

What is it that you want?

You're the one who said: we need to talk.

Fine. Finally we're talking, right?

Right. It's so good to talk, isn't it?

Stop it with the sarcasm, dammit!

The Director was losing his temper. Even with the help of the two pink tablets, his heart was pounding in his mouth. He pointed his suede-covered glove towards the constellation of freckles:

Get this into your head: this is happening. I came knocking so we could talk. I took that step. I came here unarmed. I wanted you to hear me out. I thought you wanted to hear me out. And that you might want to talk and might want me to listen. That we might want to hear what we each had to say to one another. I may not have been able to say the right things, find the precise words, but at least I tried. I made an effort. And what do I get in return? Hostility, anger, sarcasm. And this when only a few days ago you spread your legs for another man?

That's all there is to it. And count yourself lucky.

Yes, for sure. I'm a lucky cuckold, then?

You're very lucky . . . That I only spread them now, and not before. And that I only spread them for one man. So, you're a cuckold, but you only wear one horn. You're a unicorn. A mythological animal. What better luck than that?

I can't believe what you've just said.

Why?

How can you?

I'm clever.

I can't believe you said it.

The Director shook his head. His double chin surrendered in its uninterrupted fight against gravity. His jaw sagged. His shoulders gave up. It could have been said that at that very moment, the Director, who was over two metres tall, lost a few centimetres.

The Redhead shot out:

You better believe it. That's all there is to it.

No, that's where you're wrong. There's something else.

What else?

You leave me no choice.

I know: now you'll confess that you fucked the Maid right under my nose.

Don't kid yourself, you don't know everything.

And do you?

I know what I have here in my pocket.

And what do you have in your pocket? The fingers you lost?

No, your test results.

What?

Yes, your mammogram and your pap smear.

The Redhead stood up.

The Director raised the glove of authority. She stopped. There was no more space in the bedroom for the sound of crickets and cicadas.

You can sit down, the Director advised.

She did not recoil, nor did she move forward. She stretched her neck to confront him.

Don't you tell me what I can or can't do! Give me that envelope!

Shhhh. Calm down, now.

You have no right! The Blond Doctor had no right! Test results are confidential! It's my body!

The Redhead, trembling, and with tears in her eyes.

I spoke to him. I know everything.

What?

You're sick.

Noooo!

The Redhead shouted, clutching her breasts. Dropping onto the floor like an inflatable doll that someone punctured.

The Director came close.

Come, now. We need to talk. He told me you need to have the operation.

Noooo!

Yes. You'll get the operation. And you'll be well, you'll see.

Noooo!

The Director kneels.

Don't you want to live beyond one hundred?

I don't want to! They're mine!

I'll go with you. I'll be right next to you. I'll hold you. I won't let you escape, ever again.

Noooo!

But I want you to promise me one thing.

Noooo!

Promise me that, starting tomorrow, you will never again tie our Son to the piano.

How to kill a Maid: The tyranny of dust and rice

All morning she had played the role of a warrior of cleanliness. The daily battle against the tyranny of dust. She had moved the furniture. She had inspected the corners. She had climbed on a stool to open the curtains and reach the curtain rails. Kneeling on the floor, she had polished the skirting boards. She had been attentive to the smallest details. She had peered closely at things through her thick eyeglasses. Not a centimetre could escape her. Not a surface to be left unclean. Her employer, the Redhead, suffered from acute cleanliness syndrome. And she checked the thoroughness, running her finger along surfaces, like a general inspecting his troops' turnout.

The Redhead was out of breath. Eyes swollen from crying. She made a beeline for the kitchen.
    She confronted the Maid, and interrogated her:
    Why did you leave my bedroom window open?
    To let fresh air in.
    Let fresh air in?
    Yes.
    When the fresh air comes in, so will the flies and the dust.
    You're right. I'll close it. Do you need anything else?
    Boil some water.
    The Maid obeyed, interrupting her rinsing of the rice. She

struck a match. Lit the stove. Filled the kettle with water. Put the kettle on the fire. Went back to the rice.

While she judged the Maid's work, the Redhead did not miss the chance to assess the contours of her hips. The size of her thighs. The volume of her breasts. The long, hard stare of someone seeking a defect.

What are you doing?

This?

Yes.

This, here?

Yes. That there.

I'm rinsing the rice.

Rinsing the rice?

You said I must always rinse the rice before . . .

And that's how I taught you to do it?

Well . . . You said I must always rinse the rice . . .

But I didn't tell you to rinse it under the open tap, did I?

No?

Remember the butterfly?

What butterfly?

Sensitive gestures for sensitive times?

The Maid did not respond. She clutched the lilac-coloured apron. She crumpled its edges. She blushed. The circles of sweat on her blouse, beneath her armpits, grew in size and in moisture.

So?

Sorry, madam, I forgot.

Pea brain.

Sorry?

Pea brain, the Redhead repeated, and she took two steps forward and slapped the unsuspecting Maid. Her glasses flew off her head as the chords from the second and third bar floated in from the living room. The Cat, curled up in a ball of laziness beneath the kitchen table, sensed what was about to happen: it mewed and left the kitchen. It ran along the hall. Climbed the stairs. The Redhead's bedroom door was ajar. The window was wide open. And that was where the Cat jumped out. And that was where the two blue flies buzzed in.

The Maid knelt to feel around the floor tiles.
Without her glasses, the world was a blur.
Everything was far away.

On all fours, the Maid felt her way around the white floor tiles under the fulminating watch of the green eye. Without her thick eyeglasses to enlarge her world, she was defenceless. The Redhead's green eye played a game of Hot, Warm and Cold with the Maid, the iris shrinking and growing as the Maid got warmer or colder.

When the Maid's hands finally came close to the eyeglasses, the Redhead kicked them away.

So, fess up.
I said I'm sorry.
That's not what I meant. Why did you make those ginger muffins?
What?
Don't act stupid.
When?
Don't act stupid.
I don't understand.
You knew.
Me?
Don't play innocent, you stupid girl.
I'm not . . .
You made those ginger muffins on purpose!
Ginger?
Tell the truth. You knew, didn't you?
Knew what?

You put ginger in those muffins on purpose!

But the muffins . . . I swear, madam . . . I didn't . . .

The Redhead pulled the Maid by her hair. The Maid cried out. Her heart beating irregularly. As if running away. Her fingers letting go of the apron.

Didn't I tell you to make carrot muffins? So why did you make them with ginger, you silly cow?

To add flavour . . .

To add flavour . . . To add flavour . . . To give the horn, more like!

The Redhead was shouting as she grappled with an indomitable itch.

Or do you think I'm a fool? You must think I'm a fool, don't you? Don't you think I know that ginger makes men horny? Huh? You think I don't know that you're spreading your legs for the Lame Soldier . . . The one that reeks like a caged animal . . . The one hung like a horse. You think I don't know that you're fucking my husband. Huh? You stupid cow! I'm not giving you the lashing you deserve right now because the recital is coming up. But after the Government's anniversary . . . After the recital . . . Just you wait. I'll give you a good . . .

The Redhead did not finish her sentence, because the kettle whistled stridently. The Maid passed out.

Get up!

The Maid did not get up.

The Redhead bent over. She shook the still, stretched-out body. She straightened herself. She put her hands on her hips. She took the opportunity to arrange her curls and scratch her itch. She walked over to the stove. She turned the stove off. The kettle puffed. The piano lesson was approaching its end. The time was 3:4, in F minor. The two blue flies, having buzzed around the room, landed on the Maid's half-open mouth to rest and brush their legs. The Redhead shooed them off with a decisive gesture. She could not believe that the Maid had left the bedroom window open. Now it was all flies and dust, she thought. She brought her ear close to the Maid's pale mouth. She waited. Put two fingers against the carotid. She waited. Finally, she shook her head in disapproval:

The last thing we needed.

She was cooking the rice:
The telephone call

The Prison telephone exchange passes on the call.

The Director's eyes narrow. He frowns. He accepts the call. He would have expected a call from anyone other than his wife. They had not spoken in two years and now, suddenly, a conversation and a phone call.

He immediately detected a light tremor in the voice, even if the Redhead clung to her habitually abrupt and dry tone.

Hello? Hello?

Yes, it's me. What's the matter?

I need you to come home. Something happened.

Are you OK?

The Director worried that his question may have sounded too anxious.

It's the Maid.

What about her?

She died.

How?

I don't know . . . She was rinsing the rice . . . She felt ill . . . She passed out . . . Fell on the floor.

Rinsing the rice?

Yes, that's what she does . . . did.

Did she hit her head?

Who knows.

Have you checked her?

Yes.

And?

Can't hear a thing.

Yes . . . But how does rinsing rice . . . ?

How would I know? She's dead, that's it.

And our Son?

He's at the piano. We can't afford interruptions. It's the last thing we need. Only three days until the recital. If you care about that at all . . .

Of course I . . .

I didn't say anything to him. And I don't think we should, do you hear me?

He'll figure it out.

Only if you ruin everything.

He'll need to go to the kitchen.

No, no, he won't. I locked the door and then came and called you. We'll say she became ill.

The Director paused and looked at the goldfish in the fish tank.

How long ago did it happen?

Why the bloody interrogation? Is this what you do with others? Are you coming home or not?

Yes, I am. I still don't know when . . . I have something to do here . . . Don't touch anything. Leave everything as it is . . . I'll call the Tower . . . And then . . . And then . . .

He did not finish his sentence.

The Redhead hung up.

When an itch interrupts the reading

The sirens announced the change of shift.

Standing by the kitchen window, the Redhead saw the Government van pull up in front of the house. Four guards got out. They knocked on the door. After the four uniformed men had wrapped up the body in a canvas bag, they left. Death confirmed, were the only words spoken by one of them.

The Redhead got back to the window in time to see them throw the canvas bag into the van and to watch the grey vehicle gleaming as it set out towards the Factory's.

The Redhead went hurriedly through the Maid's bedroom seeking proof that the Maid and the Director had been having sex. In her search, beneath the mattress and the metal bed frame, she found a holy book and a diary. She bit her lip after the discovery. Here it was. She put the holy book to one side and sat on the bed. She turned randomly to various pages. She jumped from month to month. From a brown cross to a red cross. Impatient. She made an effort to understand the meaning of every sentence, the colour of every cross, the chronology, in her search for clues and hints. But her reading and the clarity of mind she needed to join the dots were constantly interrupted by her itch.

The Redhead gave up on reading the diary and went to find a new pot of yoghurt to fill her nether area.

Some 'X's, colours and days in the Maid's diary

X (blue) – day 9

For an hour and a half, we had weak light. I can't remember so much snow. Today I caught a glimpse of him: the Master. He stood looking at me. I've never seen such a tall man. He had to lower his head to go through doors. I'm not afraid of winter. But whatever he's hiding inside those gloves fills me with fear.

X (green) – day 17

It happened just like *He* had said it would. The wolves attacked. There can be no doubt: the Messenger knows. Nobody was expecting it. There is talk of nothing else in the City. I heard the Master saying to the Mistress that the Government is sending a group of soldiers to find the wolves. The first sign. The omen of whatever is coming next.

X (black) – day 22

Today I asked the Mistress to give me the day off because I wasn't feeling well. And I'm still not. I went to the Hospital. Passed through the Wall. To the side where the Forest is. The Doctor was nice. I took him half a dozen muffins wrapped in a tea towel. I baked them for the Lame Soldier. But his horse didn't come by today. The Doctor is handsome. The skin on his hands is soft. His fingernails are manicured. After listening to my heart, he said: your heart is weak, inflamed. And he gave me a new box of tablets. I have to take four a day. He also said I must avoid strong emotions, because I'm at risk of feeling poorly again. I'm scared. I'd rather die than go under the surgeon's knife again.

X (green) – day 3

Mistress is very demanding. She ties the Boy to the piano so he can't escape the music. The Boy is rehearsing for a recital. He plays beautifully. I see men and women within the musical landscapes he creates. Sometimes I cry when I hear him play. It reminds me of the landscapes and the men and women in my country. My heart beats faster. I take four tablets a day. It snowed, it's snowing.

X (brown) – day 16

The Messenger was arrested. It was the Lame Soldier that took him to the Prison. I'm scared of what will happen next. My brother is also scared. Our fear clings to our teeth. To our foreheads. To the insides of our eyes. But our faith is even greater. If my heart can withstand it, I'll be here when this all starts to burn.

X (red) – day 23

I was able to visit my brother in the Brown Zone. I smuggled in some pies, ginger muffins and a cream for his acne. We had the pies for dinner, drank wine and then remembered our home country and our mother. We held one another and cried. Before I left, we opened the holy book and read some passages. To cleanse ourselves of the guilt of having eaten the pies. Reading the holy book helped us digest the pies. On the way home something happened. I had wanted it for a long time, but not now and not with him. But he was so insistent that he made me think I wanted it. It was awful to discover that, in fact, I didn't really want to after having thought I did. Now I'm bleeding. I'll pray a lot tonight. With all my strength. I'll never forget those blue eyes.

X (brown) – day 25

He did something to me, and I think I have a wound inside me. I can't go to the Hospital. The Doctor will know what happened. I wrote a letter to my brother but didn't tell him what happened.

X (yellow) – day 8

For the fourth day in a row, I made lentil soup.

X (orange) – day 10

Today the Lame Soldier brought firewood. I offered him a cup of tea. He accepted. I trust him, I don't know why. I know I can't trust anyone who doesn't believe the same things I do. But I trust him, I don't know why. I asked him about the Messenger. He didn't want to say anything. He kept staring at my breasts. The Lame Soldier has a strange smell. I think it's because of the horse, but I like it. I think he also likes my smell, and my breasts. The Mistress caught us talking. I blushed from head to toes. I miss eating meat and I miss my mother. I won't be able to visit my brother tomorrow.

X (green) – day 15

My heart is a crocodile.

X (black) – day 27

I was staring at the gloves as I chopped the carrots and I cut my finger. There was a lot of blood. The Boy was tied to the piano and kept on playing. The Mistress bandaged my finger. She called me clumsy and stupid. The Master stood there watching the blood drip onto the floor. I didn't notice the blood dripping onto the floor. I could only stare at the gloves. The snow started melting.

X (blue) – day 5

Summer is here. And with the summer, also the insects. I have not seen the Lame Soldier or his horse for five days. Something happened today. I blush just to think about it: I caught the Master, in the laundry room, by the laundry basket. He was pulling knickers out of the pile of dirty laundry. Mine and the Mistress's. And then he sniffed them. Put them up to his nose, one by one. Sniffing that place where we drip.

X (yellow) – day 7

The Master asked me to shave him. As it was a beard of many years, I used the scissors first, and then the razor. My heart was beating fast. I was trembling from the fear of cutting him. He took advantage of my position and copped a feel. I pretended I hadn't noticed. Then he switched on the radio. And, while he scratched his newly shaved face, he listened to a speech by the Bald Minister.

X (black) – day 9

I'm scared of what's coming. The Master has the box. I opened the refrigerator, just to see what was inside. My God! I pray.

X (green) – day 14

Nobody speaks of anything else. They found a dead man in one of the Factory's sheds. By the stables. I prayed so hard. They found him there with two holes where his blue eyes should have been. Someone stole his blue eyes. I will never forget that blue. It was those eyes that made me do it.

X (brown) – day 20

The Little Man came to the house. I thought I'd die the

moment I saw him next to the Master. He looked at me and pretended not to know me. I tried to do the same, but I don't know if I succeeded. After, the two men went upstairs. Only four days before the Government celebrates its anniversary. And the Boy's recital. Four days before the crow caws. God give me strength. It will happen.

Tomorrow is the big day

You won't tie me up, Mother? You won't tie me up again, will you? Is that right?

Yes. You're done. I'm so proud of you. Your left hand is wonderful.

Where are you going?

To my bedroom.

You won't stay here? To listen?

Mother needs to rest. I can hear you from upstairs, in my bedroom.

Tomorrow is the recital, isn't it?

It is.

Will you be there?

In the first row.

And the Maid?

She's ill. In the Hospital. I told you already.

Oh, well . . .

But don't worry. She'll hear you too.

In the Hospital?

Yes.

But the Hospital is on the other side of the Wall . . .

The recital will be broadcast on radio.

Really?

Really.

That's good, isn't it?

It is.

Mother?
Yes.
Have you seen the Cat? He's not been around for two days . . .
He's probably gone wandering. He'll be back soon, you'll see.
Mother?
Yes.
Thank you for teaching me.
You're welcome. Tomorrow is the big day, the Redhead said.
And she shut the door.

On the other side of the door, the Redhead was shaken by an internal tremor. An old lament, from somewhere at the edges of memory, clawed at her insides. The Redhead clutched her breasts. And an inner voice whispered the most human of phrases:

We hurt most the ones we love.
    We hurt most the ones we love.
    We hurt most the ones we love.

D minor

Seated at the piano, the Son hesitates.

It is strange to play with no ropes tied to his wrists and ankles.

He looks once again at the frame hanging on the wall. In the portrait, his Father is smiling, as always. The portrait's mouth moves. The familiar voice says:

Come on. Play. You can do it.

The Son closes the book with the sheet music and shuts his long-lashed eyes. He puts his fingers on the keys. He does not need to see. His fingers know the keyboard well enough. Even in the dark, they can play the notes, they can keep the beat, they know when to pause. The muscles have a mind of their own. They stretch. Contract. Slide. Independent.

Outside, the world continues. Up above, a mad sun. Down below, the noise of life. Even further below, the singing of crickets and cicadas.

The music starts. D minor. The Son's well-trained fingers strike the keys over and over again. Harmony takes flight. It flies out the window. Flying higher and further away.

Who is hearing it?

The sentence for case 1748

There is music in the Persuasion Suite.

The radio is playing.

The Director is sitting on the purple velvet chair. Ready to sign the sentence for case 1748.

One of the most difficult and long-running cases in the Prison's history.

The Director asks the only remaining fish in the fish tank a question. The fish replies by blowing bubbles.

The Director does not understand. He holds the pen with the three fingers of his left hand. The Director decides he doesn't want to ask any more questions. Not to the fish, not to the Messenger, nor to anyone else.

And he writes in the lower corner of the case file:

Execution by firing squad.

From earth to pot, from pot to mouth

The Worker looks at himself in the mirror.

He holds a towel in his hand.

With the sun's arrival, his rebellious acne was receding in the same way that sadness receded in some people's hearts. The sun brings happiness and dries up bad skin.

The Worker puts the medicated cream on his pimples. Then he spreads a perfumed lotion on his arms and legs. His body is thin. Hairless. Lean like a marathon runner's. He rubs his fragrant fingers under his nose. And the smell gives him a jolt. He smiles. He combs back his wet fringe. He exits the bathroom.

The towel is wrapped around his waist.

As he walks along the corridor, he hears the groaning of the testy mattress coming out of the Dwarf Prostitute's apartment. His sister in faith and in secrecy. He comes close to the door. Puts his ear to the wood. Yes, inside apartment 407 the tired mattress is protesting about the insistent and frantic rhythm of fornication.

The Worker's Adam's apple rises and falls, in rhythm.

In the kitchen he slices a lemon in half. He squeezes the juice into a glass. Fills the rest with water. Drinks the lemonade. In heaven there are no lemons, he says. He opens the refrigerator door. The vegetable drawer. He spots the uncooked carrots. He chooses the thickest one. He washes it in the sink, beneath the running water. With the carrot in his mouth, he goes towards his bedroom.

Before dropping the towel onto the carpet and throwing himself naked onto the bedspread, he glances at the holy book on the chest of drawers.

Lying on the bed. Belly button facing the ceiling. He hears the noise from the streets, synchronised with the moans of fornication coming from the apartment next door. Beneath the bed is the suitcase. Inside the suitcase is a mechanism held together with wires. Tomorrow is the day, he thinks. He sucks on the carrot. He spreads his legs. Bends his knees. He curls up like a snail, bringing his knees up to his shoulders. On his left buttock, the tattooed crow twists itself over his skin. The crow wants to taste the carrot that the Worker's hand is holding like a knife.

The Worker spits into his free hand. He spreads the spit on his anus.

The carrot penetrates the Worker on his bed, just like in apartment 407 an unknown penis is penetrating the Dwarf Prostitute.

The difference is that his mattress does not complain. It is not testy.

By way of payment, that fornicating root vegetable will end up in the pot to be turned, alongside others, into a nutritious soup.

A carrot pulled out of the anus and put into the pot; then pulled out of the pot and put into the mouth. The natural process inverted.

The noises in the street diminish.

In apartment 407 the springs have stopped their creaking.

Thick semen runs down from the Worker's stomach and onto the sheets. He has tears in his eyes. He does not want to waste them. He remembers the Messenger's words. Save them for tomorrow. He swallows hard to push them back. The emotional tension does not retreat. Instead of crying, he chooses to laugh. There is no other way to release the tension: either we cry, or we laugh.

Naked, with tears in his eyes, carrot in hand, anus relaxed, the Worker laughs.

He laughs until his belly hurts from laughing.

How to look after a fish (II)

The Dwarf Prostitute climbs onto the stool and speaks to the goldfish:

All will be well, you'll see.

She had just pulled the curtains open. Daylight streams into the room. It temporarily warms the bed, empty of men. It projects shadows onto the flight of swans on the lilac-coloured wallpaper.

The Dwarf Prostitute taps on the glass with a long fingernail. On tiptoes, she leans in, looking closely at the immobile fish. It appears to be dead. She taps on the glass again. Small bubbles float to the surface and gather around the rim, like infertile eggs. She opens the jar of fish food and drops a few flakes into the fishbowl, opening her mouth to say the words:

All will be well, you'll see.

The goldfish heard her words, or perhaps felt the call of hunger – even when we are on the cusp of death, hunger calls us with its powerful voice – and struggling visibly, fin crooked, spine bent, swam tortuously, mute mouth open, no eagerness on display. It stared through the glass at the prostitute's misshaped face. It returned to the bottom of the fishbowl without eating a single crumb.

Watching it sink to the bottom and float limply over the algae-covered pebbles, its gills opening and shutting impercept-ibly to breathe, the Dwarf Prostitute cannot hold back the tears. Dirty drops of mascara fall, noisily. Concentric circles form on the surface of the water in the fishbowl, echoing her emotional distress.

The Dwarf Prostitute pulls out a handkerchief. Blows her nose. And, with smudged eyes, she confesses in a full voice, as if her heart were trying to get rid of all the feelings it never used because it lacked the courage to do so:

You little sonofabitch. You know it. It hasn't happened. But it will. Tomorrow. True. And all will be well, you'll see. Life is like that: filled with holes. The good thing is that you never got out, or will get out, of yours. You don't need to go through life as blind as a mole, as I do. Left, right. Up, down. Straight, crooked. Earth, sky. Holes and more holes . . . Not knowing when to stop, when to cover up the ones I dug blindly. Until I've dug a large pit. Or a small pit, in my case. It's always there, waiting for me to be careless. I know. You're not interested in any of this. These ordinary things. So silly of me. You don't envy, hate, judge, love. You're only interested in the flakes, aren't you, you little sonofabitch? And even when there are no flakes, you crap everywhere. You shit yourself. You shit on the flakes and on me. A fish doesn't die like God, it doesn't cry. It makes no sound. It doesn't fall into holes. It doesn't end up buried in the ground. And what I find so hard to accept in all this shitty business is that I was once a fish myself. But if there were a choice, if I had to choose between being a whore, a saint, a mole, a digger, a pit; or being a fish, never leaving its bowl, never crying or making noise, I know what I would choose. To not become a hole or dig other holes. But no. Life is not like that. And time is like a high-class whore. It has no past, and no future. And you can only fuck it in the present . . . But

all will be well, you'll see. I'm not sure how, but history is written before we start writing it. And tomorrow is the big day . . .
I'll dance for the Bald Minister in the Tower . . . I'll dance, and
the City will dance . . . But you, you won't . . . You little
sonofa . . . You won't . . . I won't allow it.

The word *allow* came out in sobs with the rest of her tears.

After taking out the handkerchief trapped in her black thigh
garter, the prostitute opens the fish-food jar and empties all its
contents into the fishbowl. Green, pink, blue and yellow flakes
tumble into the water in a rainbow-coloured cascade. She
admires the slow fall of the flakes as they begin to land, like
confetti, over the immobile goldfish with its crooked spine. And
over the pebbles at the bottom, covered in green algae bloom.

See? Despite everything. I can take care of you.

The makeup of war

The Dwarf Prostitute gets off the stool.

On the wallpaper, the white swans persist in their still flight towards the sky of the stuccoed ceiling. The sun on the bed.

The Dwarf Prostitute sits at her dressing table to retouch her war paint – lipstick, mascara, eyeshadow and eyeliner.

Makeup is a weapon of war. And a woman wearing makeup is a better prepared and more dangerous woman. She is a machine, not for killing but for seducing.

In the mirror she can see not only the makeup on her face but also the detonator and the explosives handed to her by the Worker and which, now sitting on top of the dressing table, await the *right moment* before the performance at the Government Tower.

The Dwarf Prostitute will dance for the Bald Minister. And she will carry with her a suitcase filled with instruments and accessories.

After firing up the red of her mouth, pressing the lipstick on her upper lip against her lower lip, the Dwarf Prostitute declares:

If I fall into a hole, at least I'll be looking my best.

At the right moment, the crow will caw

In apartment 408, after the morning prayer, the Worker hid the holy book under the mattress. Naked, his buttocks turned towards the mirror, he admired the tattoo. The crow on his left buttock appeared to move its beak every time he clenched his sphincter.

At the right moment, the crow will caw.

And he made his buttocks clap.

He laughed.

He got dressed. He was strangely euphoric. The big day had arrived. He approached the window and looked out onto the Factory's two chimneys, incessantly spewing their two distinct pillars of smoke – production did not stop even on a public holiday.

He said:

After today there will be no more pies.

At the Worker's feet was a suitcase. Inside it, fully prepared: the coloured wires, the mechanism's timer and the detonator for the explosives.

CAVE HOC ILLUDQUE

As soon as she walked out onto the street, the heat made her puffy and sweaty. It was hard for the makeup to remain stuck to her skin. The summer was a large yellow animal, snarling at everyone.

All her life she had been despised. All her life she had been poor and a dwarf and a mole and a whore. All her life, spat upon. But the time was coming: the time when she would finally walk tall. Thoughts of vengeance propelled her short strides. *Turn your enemies into a cobbled path for your feet. I will wait happily on my throne for the smell of devastation.* Fists clenched, high heels kicking up the dust, trampling on the heat that rose from the ground, the Dwarf Prostitute walked decisively towards the border of the Yellow Zone. In her hand was the suitcase.

The couple were waiting for her in the square with the cafés with yellow awnings. Under the shade of one of the awnings, the mother held onto the baby's pram while the father, his hand resting on her shoulder, could not look away from the obelisk with the inscription: *CAVE HOC ILLUDQUE.*

Now he understands the meaning: *BE CAREFUL WITH THIS AND THAT.*

The Dwarf Prostitute arrived, out of breath.
She did not say hello.

The father let the hand drop from the mother's shoulder. He stared at the prostitute's doll-like face.

He was handed a stamped pass and a small parcel wrapped in gold-coloured paper and ribbons – a gift of faith.

It's for your baby, said the Dwarf Prostitute, and stood on her tiptoes to look into the pram.

She smiled at the mother.

At 12:47.

All will be well.

A visit to box 1951 (I): Did grandfather use gloves?

In the corridor of the Ash Bank, the Employee turned the small key. He opened the door to safe 1951. He pulled a small metal box out of the safe. He tried to hand it to the giant with suede gloves, but the giant signalled to the Employee to give it to the Son.

The Employee obeyed.

Let me know when you're done.

And he moved away with long and fast strides.

The Son, eyes fixed avidly on the metallic cube, opened the lid as if it were a box of chocolates. Then, with a look of disappointment:

Is this Grandad?

It's what remains of Grandad, yes.

But it's dust.

These are his ashes.

He doesn't look anything like the picture we have in the living room . . .

No, he doesn't.

What did Grandad die of?

His heart.

His heart stopped working?

Yes.

Just that?

The Director nodded.

And then they put Grandad into a chimney, and he came out like this?

Yes.

Oh . . . Was Grandad good?

Sometimes.

Like you?

Like me?

Yes, sometimes you're good . . . other times . . .

You know . . . It's difficult to always be good. Sometimes you need to be bad.

But I'm good!

Yes: you're a good boy.

I don't want to be bad.

If you don't want to, you won't be. It's up to you. Ideally, you should be good very often, and bad only now and then, you understand?

I think so.

After a pause, the Son looks inside the box again:

Did Grandad wear gloves?

No.

And did he play the piano?

The Director smiled.

He liked music, but he didn't play the piano. Grandad would have wanted me to be a pianist. But I think he passed this desire onto you instead.

Mother also likes music a lot. She knows how to play the piano. But she doesn't. She stopped playing to teach me, didn't she?

She did. After you were born, she never again . . . Her talent was also passed onto you.

Grandad was an engineer, wasn't he? Didn't he work for the Government? And now he's here, in this box.

Yes . . . Do you know what an engineer does?

An engineer builds things.

Very good.

Grandad built our City's Wall, didn't he?

That's right. And do you know what the Government is?

The Government ordered him to build the Wall. The Government rules over everyone in every home. The Government rules over the pies and over the Factory. The Government orders the walls of every house to be painted. The Wall, the Factory, the Tower, they're all important to the Government, aren't they?

They are.

The Wall protects us from wolves. And the Factory gives us the pies. But Mother won't let us eat too many pies.

That's right.

When I'm older, I don't want to be an engineer.

What do you want to be?

I want to be a man. And to wear gloves like you.

A visit to box 1951 (II): This is why Father wears gloves

The Director swallowed hard. He was overcome by anguish. He leaned down towards the Son and gave him a stern look:

No! You don't need gloves!

But I want . . .

No, you don't . . . You don't need gloves. You're a pianist. You have strong and beautiful fingers.

But I can play with gloves.

No, you can't. Gloves make you lose sensitivity and strength.

But your fingers are strong, aren't they?

They are not as strong as yours.

Is that why you don't hold my hand?

The Director did not reply.

The Son, eyes glued on his Father, insisted:

Why do you use gloves, Father?

To keep my hands clean.

Because of your work?

Yes. I don't like having dirty hands.

Is that it?

Yes.

But you're not working now, and Mother told me to wash my hands before leaving home. They're clean, you see?

The Director's heart could not withstand the assault of guilt-free love. In that metallic and sterile hallway, surrounded by the dead turned to dust, he kneeled and hugged the Son. No longer worrying about *the loss*, he pulled the suede glove off his left hand and ran his three remaining fingers through the boy's mussed-up hair. He kissed him on the forehead. On the face. Many times. The Son, pressed against the Director, was still holding the metal box containing the grandfather's remains. In the middle of the hug, some of the ashes (parts of the grand-father) fell out of the box and onto the corridor floor, without the Son or the Director noticing, busy as they were opening their hearts.

After letting go, the Director put the glove back on in front of the Son's amazed eyes.

See, this is why I have to wear gloves.

Oh . . . You don't have them all!

I only have three.

You're missing the little finger and the thumb. What about the other hand?

Same.

That's why you can't play the piano.

It is.

How did you lose them? Did a wolf attack you in the Forest?

Sort of. It was a wolf, but not in the Forest.

So?

Your father played cards against a wolf and lost.

At cards?

Yes. But now your father played the wolf again and won.

You won!

Yes.

You're telling tales, aren't you?

You like stories, don't you?

But I don't like stories with wolves.

Nor do I. But we can't pretend they don't exist.

After a pause, the Son takes the Director's incomplete hand.

But did you win? Really?

I won.

So, it means you'll have new fingers?

Yes, sort of. But you'll have to promise not to tell anyone.

It's our secret?

It is. Now we have a secret.

Good. But you still won't hold my hand, will you?

Yes, I will . . . Now, say goodbye to Grandad. We have to find the Cat before we go up into the Tower.

Fine.

He dipped five of his elegant fingers, which would shortly be playing the piano in the ballroom with the lustrous chandelier, into the metallic box from safe 1951.

They picked at the grey dust, delicately touching the grandfather's remains.

89-167-2-23-6-14-6440-3-2-5-1-17-574/
21-4-3-8-12:47

While the Director and the Son climbed the 89 steps of the staircase in the Grey Zone's Ash Bank, hand in hand, the executioner known as Glass Eye, now with a new eye, blue like a deep river, to replace his glass one, coughed for the last time in the Hospital's room 167. While the Worker made his way down to the second floor of building 23 in the Brown Zone, the Dwarf Prostitute was stepping out of the Government Tower's lift on the sixth floor. While the Messenger ran around the perimeter of the Prison patio, asking himself why he had been dreaming about a seagull in the Forest for the past fourteen nights, the Maid's ashes were being swept out of the Factory oven and into a metallic box with the number 6440. While the Small Man ate three meat pies, sitting at a table in the Club, the Blond Doctor was buying two pairs of gloves in a shop in the Brown Zone's 5th Street, and the executioner known as Neck Brace was taking off his neck brace, sitting in the purple velvet chair inside the Persuasion Suite, the better to open his mouth and swallow the live goldfish. While the Lame Soldier climbed off the saddle of his tall horse to take seventeen unsteady steps, the Assistant walked into the Bald Minister's office carrying a printed copy of Law 574/21 under his arm. While the Secretary with the black eyeliner changed her sanitary pad for the fourth time that day, the Bald Minister was fastening the third button of his white shirt. All of this was happening while the Redhead walked across the square towards the Government Tower, and for the eighth time that day squeezed and adjusted her breasts.

The Redhead heard the Cat's familiar mewing. She looked around. By the side of the road was a baby's pram. The Redhead approached it. She leaned into the pram. That was where the mewing came from. There was no baby. She took the Cat in her arms. The Cat was trembling with fear. For no reason, the Redhead pulled away the blanket with her right hand, her fingernails painted purple.

A digital clock displayed the red numbers:

12:47

Winning the disaster

In the roulette of disasters, in the casino of days, the ball is in play. Going round in circles. Respecting the universe's central rule: terrible things resist the passage of time.

We have placed all our chips on a certain number and a certain colour. While the roulette is spinning vertiginously, we bite our nails. The ball jumps from one number to another, one colour to another, insect-like in its restlessness: 14, red, 27, black. Forced to place a bet – whoever is alive has to gamble – we place our chips on 23, red. The roulette continues spinning and the ball (the insect) becomes tired of hopping. We cannot bear to watch. And after biting our nails we are nibbling on our own flesh. Then, gravity or chance finally play their part: the ball stops, the insect bites, and many lose.

Although we play the game every day, although we spit in the face of fate to seduce Lady Luck, we don't know whose is the hand that makes the roulette spin, nor whose are the fingers that collect the chips.

And who wrote the rules of fear?

Do we smile or whistle in the face of our neighbour's misfortune?

Or do we give up, leave the room before the game is finished, wearing an elegant suit but with our underpants soiled?

And now: which is the most powerful force?

Gravity or chance?

The soothsaying leg (II)

The first explosion happened before the agreed time and in the wrong place. It had not gone according to plan. Something got in the way: some little pebble stuck in the machinery of rebellion. Chance and accident do not belong in the realm of mathematics, but in the realm of the unknown. And only a few are able to anticipate or foresee, and they take us by the hand to somewhere unsuspected; and worse, when we arrive, and look around, we realise that that is not the place where we wanted to be.

Outside the Wall, the radiant yellow morning bursts into the dark spaces that night had inhabited. Flies and mosquitoes buzz dementedly through the sun-chewed air in search of territories to conquer when, in the Brown Zone's building 23, the Worker comes down the back staircase with suitcase in hand and heart beating fast.

The suitcase is heavier than usual. Concealed within it, besides the usual smock and packed lunch, are the wires, the clock, the detonator and the explosives.

After the final turn opening out onto the landing, the Worker runs hurriedly and unexpectedly into the Lame Soldier who, with a boot on the first step, had just begun his ascent. The Lame Soldier's eyes widen with surprise but he hardly budges. His gun, hanging from his shoulder by a leather strap, swings like a pendulum. The Worker, much less robust, gives a small, unbalanced hop, crashing against the wall, and the suitcase flies out of his hands like a bird, only to land on the step where the Lame Soldier's freshly shined boots mirror the shadows around them.

Looking at the Worker, the Lame Soldier noted the oily, acne-covered skin. The sight of that face, dented by pimples and pustules, was repellent.

The Lame Soldier waited for an apology, but no sound came out of the Worker's lips. With his back to the wall, his eyes remained nervously glued to the suitcase. On top of which the shiny boot containing the *soothsaying leg* was already planted commandingly.

The Worker and the Lame Soldier remained static, silent, measuring each other up. Casting suspicious looks at one another, trying to get under the other's skin. To arrive at the heart of fear.

Summer was burning and breaking through walls. If the two men had not been so focussed on avoiding a tumble after their encounter, they might have been able to hear the singing of the crickets and cicadas coming from kilometres beyond the Wall, penetrating every space. But now, along with the dehydrating heat, there was only the excitement of molecules arising from the unexpected near-collision, and the aerial dance of two blue flies.

The two men were sweating. For similar reasons. With neither of them knowing what was going through the other's mind, their pores did not secrete the same smell but were twinned in their identical desires. One had descended the stairs thinking about every step of the plan so that his explosion would happen simultaneously with the others, at the agreed time. The other was getting ready to climb the stairs, to knock on the door of apartment 407, where the gaping wet mouth of the tiny prostitute would welcome the liquid shrapnel of his own internal explosion.

In the end, great changes, whether astronomical or climatic, natural or social, the ones that change the direction of events on Earth or in the universe, occur because of explosions.

The Worker moved towards the steps where the Lame Soldier's shadow was falling. With a single movement of his shoulder, the Lame Soldier used his weapon to block him from passing. Pain was once again gnawing at his leg. Something big was coming. Something fierce. He pointed his gun at the Worker.

The two blue flies interrupted the silence with their tireless chase. Oblivious to the dangerous circus taking place in front of them, they landed on the Worker's head. They made his slicked-back blond hair their marital bed. The wax that held his hair together made a very attractive and fragrant berth.

Even as he looked down, the Worker could see the rifle's barrel pointed at one of his eyes. And, in a ridiculously high-pitched and sweet voice, he asked:

Can I have that suitcase?

What kind of voice is that?

Can I please have the suitcase? The sirens have sounded. I can't be late.

What the hell? That voice doesn't match your face. You have the face of a murderer, but the voice of a whore. Where did you get a face like that? It makes me sick.

The Worker put his hand on his hair to push his fringe off his eyes. The gesture scared off the blue flies, now stuck together. They buzzed off like comets before resuming their copulation.

Can I have the suitcase? I have my smock and my lunch. Without the smock I can't . . .

So, let's have a look at what you have. I'm feeling a little peckish.

. . . work at the Factory.

What do you do there?

I'm a butcher.

Is that right?

I slice the animals open and pull out their insides.

Do you have any pies in the suitcase?

No, we're not allowed to eat them.

You poor thing. You're not allowed to eat the pies? Cut the crap and open the fucking suitcase!

The Lame Soldier put his index finger on the trigger. The Worker did not obey and did not lower his head. His hair wax was melting.

He passed his hand over his oily forehead, but his gaze remained fixed. As if he were fixing with his sight something beyond the Lame Soldier, beyond the brown walls, beyond the Wall, somewhere in the other half of the world. His pupils glinted unexpectedly while the flies continued to engage in their intense copulation.

I know you.

Is that right? Where from?

Here.

Have we crossed paths before?

I live across from 407.

Oh, so you're a neighbour of that little whore . . . Do you also turn tricks?

You're the one who arrested the Messenger.

I'm a soldier, I just do my job. But tell me: do you turn tricks as well? Do you like men?

Depends on how much they pay me.

How much do you want?

Having asked the question, the Lame Soldier laughed. And the Worker responded with his own laughter. The laughter climbed up the staircase. Even the flies were laughing, though surely they had good reasons to be laughing. The Worker's hair was a much better place to copulate in than the crusty eyes or the fidgety tail of the horse where they had tried to settle earlier.

The two men exchanged long peals of laughter, showing their enamelled teeth.

But within the underpants of one and the other, blood was rushing to their cocks in explosive bursts.

Ignoring the pain of his *soothsaying leg*, the Lame Soldier asked:

How long would it take for us to go upstairs?

The suitcase, please?

Is that the only thing you want?

Yes.

And what would you do in exchange?

Whatever you tell me to do.

Is it valuable to you?

It's mine.

So, come here.

The Worker's head came close to the Lame Soldier's trousers, guided by the eye of the rifle's barrel. Amid all the excitement, the flies concluded their nuptial mating and, dizzied and excited, flew past the rifle barrel in search of daylight.

With the sole of the boot on his good leg, the Lame Soldier pushed the suitcase over to the Worker.

Very well, my pimply-faced friend . . . Open that suitcase quickly . . . Then we can go upstairs.

Before opening the suitcase, the Worker stared at the Lame Soldier and, amid euphoric laughter, said:

It's happening, now.

A horse does not lose its elegance

Various shots were heard followed by an explosion. Shouts like howls. It was the big day. The Government was celebrating its anniversary and the celebration cake had been baked by the most experienced bakers in the Government Tower. Celebrations and festivities were expected all around the City. There was even going to be a piano recital in the ballroom with the lustrous chandelier.

Facades and gables were decorated with wildflowers and with blue flags with the Government star. On the streets, smiles on faces. Peering out of windows, eyes filled with hungry curiosity.

But that explosion was not in the script.

After the detonation, rubble and dust rained down by the railing. The Lame Soldier's horse neighed over and over again. It kicked wildly, performing a scared dance. Its wild eyes bulging in their sockets, its front legs shooting up into a suddenly reddened sky. The fire was devouring anything that could be devoured in the brown building, and was spreading. But a horse does not lose its elegance. Every one of its movements, even the roughest and most sudden, looked beautiful, in contrast with the scene of fresh devastation.

The horse continued neighing and kicking, its hoofs crashing in a loud dance. Until a moment later, when the disorderly clacking of military boots could already be heard in the distance, the reins loosened from the railings and the horse, now free, galloped away towards the Wall.

Despite the empty saddle, it did not gallop alone. Protected by the horse's undulating mane, two blue flies, parasitic and entertained, were riding it. Happy flies, rubbing the legs and wiping the eyes that, for reasons they could not understand, almost by chance, had been spared at the start of the disaster.

Acknowledgements

To my parents.

To Zé Louro, Rui Cabrita, Afonso Cruz and Nélio Conceição.

To Zeferino Coelho and Alberto Manguel.

To Rachmaninoff and all the authors and books whose words seeped into these pages.

Thank you.